MW01230186

To Dance with an Angel

DAN BARNWELL

To Dance with an Angel
Copyright © 2022—Dan Barnwell

All rights reserved. This book is protected by the copyright laws of the United States of America. This book may not be copied or reprinted for commercial gain or profit. The use of short quotations or occasional page copying for personal or group study is permitted and encouraged. Permission will be granted upon request.

ISBN: 9798844095801 (paperback)

Foreword

THIS STORY IS ABOUT A boy who is autistic. What causes autism is a mystery, a question that is discussed, and very often argued between doctors and parents. It is considered to be a lifelong disability, appearing in early childhood. There are no typical cases because there are no typical humans.

Every child, every human being who is affected by autism is a complete living soul trying to experience the adventure of life. The lens through which they view the world may seem to be out of focus. Social interaction can be confusing. A life of repetition and daily habit often best suits their mindsets and eases their difficulties when dealing with emotions.

They are people. They want to participate. They want to communicate. They want to accomplish. They want to discover their own talents and develop them. When family members are watching at exactly the right time and suddenly see that spark of talent, that amazing natural ability, they will use up all of the patience in the universe helping that little spark become a bright shining light.

It is not all of a sudden that some miracles happen.

Chapter One

IT WAS A SUNNY JUNE day when Jonathan Picasso Higgins and Laura Dell Ashe were married at the First Baptist Church of Cedar Ridge. They were a little young to be getting married, maybe. He was twenty one and she was only eighteen years old. But if they were a little young, they were also a lot in love and had been that way for four solid years.

Jonathan, who has been called J. P. since he was a child, was one of the Higgins boys. They were an old Irish American family whose fathers for generations had taken to giving their sons extravagant names of famous people. It was because, they said, their surname Higgins was so plain and old and Gaelic. So he was Jonathan the friend of King David and Picasso, the artist. Of course, like all of those who had been born before him, he went by his initials. That's what they always did, because of their Irish ancestry.

Laura Dell, on the other hand, was called by both names even when she wasn't getting into trouble. Her straight black hair and dark eyes left no doubt about her American Indian ancestry. She stood tall and straight and her smile was like a hypnotizing charm when she was happy. But her eyes could turn into black gun barrels if you made her mad and J. P. knew it.

They were a beautiful and happy young couple and everybody in Cedar Ridge loved them. They began as most of us begin. There was a little rented house on a side street three blocks from Highway 22, which is the only main road that passes through Cedar Ridge. J. P. worked as an electrician apprentice and Laura Dell was a dental assistant.

For this young couple, married didn't mean bored. They paddled down the creeks around the area and camped on sand bars. Sometimes they ate too many hot dogs and sometimes they drank a few too many beers. That was during the warmer months. During the winter, if it wasn't too awfully cold, they sat by their fire pit in the backyard and ate too many hot dogs and drank too many beers there. Laura Dell couldn't drink much at all because, you know, she was part Indian. And J. P. couldn't keep his smart mouth shut because he was part Irish. He claimed that Laura Dell could hear a beer can open and her speech would be slurred. She said that J. P. would start telling some stupid lie about an event which had never happened before he swallowed his first swig.

So, most weekends were filled with fun parties and friends on Saturday nights and grouchy cleanups and hangovers on Sundays. They saved a little money and they wasted a little money and paid their bills with the rest. Somehow they finished growing up together and loved each other even more after every argument and after every fun time as well.

This type of life went on for a couple of years and, to tell the truth, they didn't mature very much. Then one night at the fire pit in the backyard, when everyone was having a good time, a husband kissed a wife. It's the same old story over and over. The husband wasn't married to that wife, and it didn't look like it was the first time they had ever kissed. Only, this time they were drunk and they kissed each other in front of the husband who that particular wife was married to.

It is a very bad thing to combine infidelity with alcohol and fire. The husband who had been wronged fully intended to beat the man who had kissed his wife to death. The husband who had kissed the wrong wife wanted to stay alive.

This was not a shouting fight. There was no cursing or accusing. This was two young strong men at war. It was powerful and bloody with hard accurate punches. After several hard licks, they grabbed a hold and began to wrestle. This gave the other friends a chance to separate them, but they moved too slowly. One of the combatants hooked a heel against a rock beside the fire pit and they both fell into the fire.

Fire and sparks puffed up in an orange ball. There was screaming and the smell of burning hair and flesh.

Within a few seconds the men were pulled from the coals, but oh, those awful seconds. The friends lay side by side, the one still cursing the other as they both trembled in pain.

Someone turned a hose on both of them because orange embers smoldered in what clothes they still had left. A blanket was thrown into the bed of a pickup truck. Each person was wrapped in a separate blanket and they all took off for the hospital fifteen miles away.

Almost everybody had been burned. At the hospital, the two who had fallen into the fire were quickly pushed into the treatment area while the rest were treated in the emergency room lobby.

J. P.'s hands were a mess and Laura Dell had a burn between her wrist and elbow on one arm.

Sunday morning was dawning as she drove home. J. P. sat in the passenger's seat, weeping great heartfelt sobs. He held his bandaged hands in front of his face, moaning and crying, wordless groans of pain. When they finally made it home, they fell together on the couch and held each other as close as they could without touching a burned place.

Laura Dell dozed for an hour and when she woke up, J. P. wasn't on the couch with her. She found him in the backyard beside the fire pit. He was gathering beer cans and other trash, putting them into a large trash bag. She could tell that his hands were hurting every time he picked something up and bagged it.

"Sweetheart," she whispered.

J.P. looked up, his eyes full of pain, "Help me," was all he said, and she helped him. Every little piece of plastic, every patch of burned clothing, every can was found and bagged. Still, the presence of disaster filled their senses.

"Let's go in and drink a cup of coffee," she said, and J. P. followed her. They walked stoop shouldered like a couple who had aged in one miserable night, and truly they had.

They sat together on the back step, sipping their coffee as a cold winter sun tried to brighten a pitiful day. J. P. said, "Laura Dell, I think it's time to grow up. I don't want to be stupid anymore. I don't want to be wasteful anymore. I don't want to ever drink anything again."

Laura Dell smiled a bitter smile. "You read my mind. No more parties."

J. P. had tears pouring from his eyes again. "My friends," he whispered, his voice cracking. He shook his head and looked at the fire pit, remembering every second from the night before. Laura Dell scooted closer against him.

"You can't undo it, J. P." She laid her head against his shoulder and they crossed that sad, final bridge into adulthood together.

Chapter Two

THE COUPLE WERE SURPRISED HOW much of a difference the absence of alcohol made in their lives. First, weekends cost less, and an entire day is added as well. Sunday begins at least two hours earlier. So they started going to church, which added to the joy they found in simple pleasures, like afternoon naps, and cuddling up and watching television, and planting a backyard garden. It seemed that the more they were together, the more they enjoyed each other's company. So it was no surprise to either of them when Laura Dell sat in J. P.'s lap one evening and whispered, "What do you like better, Daddy or Papa?"

J. P. grinned real big and whispered back, "I kind of like Papa, now that the decision needs to be made."

Laura Dell leaned her head across his neck and smiled and said, "I like Papa, too. So you're going to be a Papa in about seven months."

And J. P. said, "Good. I want to be one."

The baby was due in April, the month when everything seems to find new life, so Laura Dell and J. P. spent the winter months watching the baby bump grow in her belly. When the time came to discover what the baby would be, they were both happy to learn that the new addition to their family was going to be a little baby boy.

Laura Dell made sure that she ate good food and got plenty of sunshine and exercise. She took the required vitamins and she worked through her eighth month. After that, she couldn't lean over the dental patients, so her employer gladly allowed her to take a few months off.

So it was that through the month of March, Laura Dell watched the gray of winter begin its change to green and she felt the cold wind give way to warm spring rain and sun. On April fourteenth, Easter Sunday morning at four o'clock, she sat up suddenly in the bed and said, rather loudly, "J. P.!"

They had everything packed in a suitcase. Her medical information was laid on top of the dresser in a folder. There was a make up bag with all of her necessary items, plus a toothbrush and toothpaste beside the bathroom sink.

J. P. helped Laura Dell get her gown wrapped around her. This was accomplished with her sitting down some of the time and standing up some of the time. Every slight movement was followed by a loud moan from Laura Dell, "Ohhhhh!"

J. P. ran out to the car and opened the passenger side door and leaned the seat back about half way. He wondered if he should lean it all the way back. No, half way, he could let it back farther if Laura Dell was uncomfortable. He didn't want her to fall back too far and start hurting worse than she already was.

He scooted back into the house, grabbed Laura Dell by the shoulder, and they stumbled along side by side through the door. When she sat down in the car seat, the angle was perfect and J. P. blew out a great big long sigh.

"What's wrong?" Laura Dell asked between gritted teeth.

"Nothing's wrong. Something went right."

J. P. hopped into the driver's seat and started the car. Laura Dell looked at him, her eyes all squenched up. "My bags, J. P."

"Oh, yeah, the bags." He ran back into the house and came back with the suitcase and make-up bag and threw them into the back seat. When he opened the driver's door to get in, she said, "Medical folder."

Back he went, and back he came with the folder. He sat down in the driver's seat and handed Laura Dell the folder. When he turned the headlights on and put the car in reverse, he said, "Crap! The font door is standing wide open." He tried to get out of the car, but it was still in reverse and he was barely able to get his foot on the brake pedal before he was knocked down. After getting his balance, he put the car in park and ran to the door and slammed it shut. When J. P. got back to the car, Laura Dell was laughing and crying and groaning and trying not to say too many cuss words.

"Boy, you better stop flopping around and get me to the hospital or I am going to have this baby right here in this driveway. Ohhh! Aahahah! Ohhh."

J. P. calmed down as he drove and even though Laura Dell's pains increased in frequency and became worse, he was steady and in charge by the time they made it to the emergency room.

The staff at the hospital were efficient. This was not the first woman in labor they had ever met. Laura Dell's doctor was there in fifteen minutes. Everything was going smoothly. Between pains J. P. whispered words of love and comfort as he squatted by the bed and held her hand tightly. The doctor and two nurses were getting everything ready when all of a sudden, Laura Dell asked, "What happened? Did the power go off?"

The doctor turned quickly and looked at Laura Dell's eyes. "Blood pressure!?" One of the nurses gave her head a quick shake, no. The other nurse took a firm grip on J. P.'s arm and whispered, "Let's get you out for a few minutes." She pulled hard and J. P. let Laura Dell's hand slide from his.

As he went through the door into the lobby, he asked the nurse, "What's wrong? What happened?"

"I'm not sure. We'll let you know in a few minutes. Wait out here."

J. P. stood by the door, alone. Everything, everyone that was his life was on the other side of that door and he didn't know if they were....

He found a public phone. He called his pastor. He

called his parents. He called Laura Dell's parents. He told them to come to the hospital, to hurry, that something was wrong. He didn't know what, please hurry. And they came. In just a few minutes, the waiting area was filled with family members, and the preacher, and half a dozen of those elderly prayer warriors who pray to God first, before anything else. J. P. got down on his knees, weeping and begging God not to take her, not to take their baby. The congregation circled around him and settled in for a quiet vigil. An elderly lady stood up and said, "Not today, death! Today is a day of birth. Today is the day for life. Today is Resurrection Day and death has no place here. Not today, not today, in the name of the Great Healer Jesus Christ, not today!"

Suddenly, the sound of a baby crying could be heard from the delivery room! Everyone stood still, not even taking a breath. J. P. walked slowly, almost floating down the hall. Just as he came to the delivery room door, a nurse pushed it open. She was holding a tiny bundle of soft blanket and inside that blanket was the beautiful little baby boy. The nurse held him out so J. P. could see his little purple red face.

J. P. felt dizziness try to pull him off balance and he braced against the closest wall. Finally, he took a deep breath, "Where's my wife?"

"She's having a little bit of a problem with her blood pressure. We had to do a c-section to save the baby."

"Laura Dell!" J. P. tried to push the door open, but the nurse blocked him.

"Mr. Higgins, your wife has been moved to a room. She's going to be okay. We wanted you to see your son first before we take him to the nursery. Your wife will be able to see him in a few hours. Here, sit down and hold your son. Let your family see him, just not too close."

J. P. found a chair and sat. The nurse handed the baby over to his trembling hands. The congregation and family gathered around and said things like, "Look at that head full of black hair." and, "Look at those eyes. He's already looking around!"

J. P. told them, "Laura Dell has been moved to a room. They had to take the baby out. The nurse said she should be okay in a few hours."

The pastor said a prayer of intense gratitude. Everybody except J. P. and the two sets of grandparents left, some wiping tears, others smiling with their arms around each other. The nurse came out and took the baby. She told them what room Laura Dell was in and the family all headed for the elevator.

At the door of the room, J. P. hesitated. On the other side of that door was the only person he had ever felt a romantic love for, and he had almost lost her. But he had not lost her, and he pushed the door open and took three giant steps to be beside her. She raised a feeble trembling hand and he grabbed it and kissed it. "My love," he whispered, "My Laura Dell."

She smiled, still so very weak, so sleepy. "Where's that baby?"

"They took him to the nursery. Oh, Laura Dell, he is

so beautiful. Did you see him?"

"Only for a second, but I heard him. I knew he had a voice."

The grandparents gathered around them and whispered words of love as they should have done. Nobody talked about the sudden crisis right then. It wasn't the time.

J. P.'s father finally asked the question, "What are y'all going to name that boy?"

"His name," said J. P., "is Michael Angelo Higgins."

Laura Dell's mother said, "Lord have mercy," and then she put her hand over her mouth and blushed.

Laura Dell said, "J. P., that's all one name. Michaelangelo is just one long name."

But J. P. smiled a smug looking smile and said, "Our son's name is Michael Angelo, two names, Michael Angelo Higgins."

Chapter Three

AFTER TWO DAYS IN THE hospital, the baby came home, and he brought his mother with him. Family and friends came by to see the baby and, of course, to check on the mother. Michael Angelo was looking around from the moment he landed in his new home. "Look at those eyes," J. P. would say. "He's exploring already. I think he's going places for sure."

Michael Angelo did seem to be a stout baby. He was moving his head and arms constantly. By the time he was two weeks old, he was reacting to sounds and sudden movement. He squeezed fingers and held on to blankets, everything that babies normally do. To Laura Dell and J. P., he did all of those things amazingly well. The first time he laughed out loud, they thought it was a miracle.

"Oh, you're such a big boy!" Laura Dell would say when she picked him up. He was solid muscle. When he was four months old, he was scooting around on his belly and when he was six months old, he started crawling. He loved to hear music, smooth music, music with a melody. He would coo to the blended harmony of voices. Laura Dell could put him in his walker and give him a plastic spoon and turn on the radio and Michael Angelo would hop and bang that spoon and scoot around for an hour totally content.

When J. P. would come home from work, he was never too tired to scoop Michael Angelo up in his arms and dance around the living room with him, singing and laughing. But Michael Angelo didn't laugh when they were dancing. He turned his head to whatever direction J. P. moved and floated along as if he was the king of the whole wide world. To that baby, dancing was something important. It was serious.

Now, the Higgins family was an ordinary family. Most of them were skilled in some trade, but few were so exceptional that they received a special public notice. However, every so often, a particularly talented child would be born, who would grow up to be a noted athlete, or performer of some kind, even an occasional statesman had come from the family. The special children like these always shared a noticeable trait. They were all left handed.

That was why J. P. made such a big deal out of it when Michael Angelo started holding things in his left hand. At about nine months, he started throwing things. They say that babies teach themselves depth perception by dropping their toys and throwing them. If that's true,

Michael Angelo wanted to know how far away something across the room was. He was strong! He laughed at the sound of one solid object hitting another one. Leave him alone and everything in the room that he could reach and he could lift would become a flying object.

"He's going to be a quarterback! He's going to be a pitcher!" J. P. would declare to anybody who happened to be in the room when Michael Angelo would launch a toy across the room.

When he started walking, his day was often spent scurrying around looking for something to beat like a drum or something to throw. Almost all of his toys were soft and he had every size of rubber ball that was made.

Laura Dell knew that the banging around and ball throwing were nothing exceptional. She was glad that her baby was healthy. To her, Michael Angelo was special because of the way he heard music. He seemed to show little interest in the thumpity thump of children's songs on the television. The bang and squeal of rock wasn't recognized by him as music at all. But let him hear the smooth call of a violin and the power of a combo of brass horns along with a harmony of voices and he moved to the rhythm as he played. He hummed along with any song, staying on key even before he ever spoke an understandable word. In this, Laura Dell saw a grace and a talent in her child.

When he was a year old, their doctor scheduled a day for Michael Angelo to get what everyone calls the baby shots. The pediatrician, Doctor Williams, told Laura

Dell, "Now, he may run a low grade fever for a day or so after he gets these, but that's to be expected. If he gets too hot, though, I want you to bring him in, alright?"

Laura Dell said that she would. When they got home from the doctor's office, the baby didn't seem to be feeling any effects from the shots at first. He didn't eat much supper and he went right to sleep after he had his evening bath. Laura Dell touched his forehead and his belly before she lay down for the night and he was a little warm, but the doctor had said that was not a cause for alarm.

Who knows what happens inside a little child's body when medicine that is acceptable to almost every baby's system is not acceptable to this certain one?

The next morning Laura Dell found Michael Angelo standing in his crib. She only noticed it a little bit when he didn't reach for her when she picked him up. He seemed so still when she changed him from his pajamas to his day clothes. Maybe he will perk up after he has breakfast, she thought. But he ate as though he was still half asleep, not tasting or smacking. He didn't grab at the spoon or playfully bite down on it.

When Laura Dell put him in the floor, he just stood there. He looked around as if he was in a strange place, not picking up his toys, not walking anywhere, not doing anything. He stood still, doing nothing.

Laura Dell whispered, "Michael Angelo." The baby didn't respond. She clapped her hands to make sure he could hear. He turned and looked at her, but his face was blank. She got one of his favorite balls and handed it to him. Again, he looked at her, his eyes empty. He didn't reach for the ball.

Laura Dell's heart jumped in her chest. "Michael Angelo!" she called louder, but he stood still. "Baby!" she said even louder now, panic in her voice. Still, there was no response. "Oh, my God, no! What's wrong with my baby? What's wrong with my baby?"

She ran for the telephone and called the office where J. P. worked. J. P. was not at the office. "Will you please find him and tell him to meet me at the doctor's office? Something's happened to the baby."

"Mrs. Higgins, he will probably call in at lunch, can it wait until then?"

"No! I am leaving right now for the doctor's office and somebody better be leaving right now going to find my husband, do you understand? Something has happened to our baby and you need to find him and tell him now!"

"Yes ma'am, Mrs. Higgins. If I have to, I will go find him myself."

"Thank you, so much. Tell him that I am on my way to the doctor with Michael Angelo."

Laura Dell picked up Michael Angelo and headed for the doctor. As she drove, she whispered, "Oh, please, dear God, please let my baby be alright." But deep in her heart, she knew her baby. She knew that her baby was not alright.

Chapter Four

WHEN LAURA DELL CAME INTO the doctor's office, she walked to the desk holding her baby. "Something's wrong with him," she told the receptionist.

When a person has worked several years at the front desk for a pediatrician, she learns to trust a mother's instincts. "Bring him right on back, Mrs. Higgins," she said. "I'll get Dr. Williams immediately." She opened a door to a treatment room and Laura Dell sat down on the padded seat. The receptionist disappeared down the hall, walking swiftly.

J. P. stepped into the little room within a few minutes. "What happened?" he asked, his face pale.

"Michael Angelo can't wake up, J. P." Laura Dell's voice rose as she talked, "I fed him. I tried to play with him. He's not there anymore, J. P. He's gone somewhere and he can't find his way back. Oh, my baby! My poor lost little baby!"

J. P. took Michael Angelo from her hands. "Hey, Buddy," he whispered. "Hey, Mikey, do you see Papa?"

Michael Angelo didn't move, didn't put his arm over J. P.'s shoulder like he always did. He didn't look at his Papa's eyes and smile like he usually did. He didn't react in any of the ways that a one year old baby naturally does.

J. P. held the baby out at arm's length. "Michael Angelo. Look at Papa." J. P. gave a soft whistle. Michael Angelo didn't react. He handed the baby back to Laura Dell. "Has he been crying like he's hurting anywhere?"

"No, he hasn't done anything. He's gone, J. P. Our baby's gone." She held Michael Angelo against her chest, sobbing.

"He's not gone. He just doesn't feel good. Doctor Williams will give him some medicine and he'll be fine." J. P. sat down beside her and rubbed her shoulders. "Doctor Williams will find out what's wrong. He'll know what to do."

They sat there together, Laura Dell crying, J. P. trying to quiet her, Michael Angelo as still as a stone, doing nothing at all.

Finally, Doctor Williams came in, a calm smile on his face. A nurse stood slightly beside and behind him. "Now, let's see what's going on with Michael Angelo this morning," he said as he took the baby. As soon as he lifted him, Laura Dell noticed a slight change in the doctor's smile.

The doctor checked the baby's eyes and ears, took his temperature, felt his thighs and calves and shoulders and belly. He listened to his heart and lungs.

"Humph," he said. He turned to the nurse and said, "Let's get a blood sample, okay? As soon as you have something, bring it to me."

The doctor looked at J. P. "Y'all just wait right here. I'll be back in a few minutes." And he went out through the door. The nurse drew a blood sample and whispered that she would be right back. Laura Dell and J. P. were left to sit and wait again.

After a long thirty minutes, the doctor and the nurse came back. Neither of them were smiling. Doctor Williams sat down on a stool and scooted in close. "Michael Angelo's white count is up a little bit, but that is not unexpected because he had that shot yesterday. His temperature is at one hundred, but that's not really high. His eyes and ears look great and everything else seems to be healthy."

J. P. said, "Knock it off, Doctor. I think you have an idea about what's wrong. You need to tell us. You need to tell us now. And don't give us any sugar coated bull."

Doctor Williams looked at the floor. His shoulders slumped. His whole body seemed to shake as he gave a long, sad sigh. "I think your baby.... I think Michael Angelo may have had a reaction to his shots from yesterday."

J. P. stood up quickly. "A reaction? What kind of a reaction? What's a reaction mean? What have you done? What have you done to our child?" There was fire in J. P.'s eyes. There was fear in his heart, and sadness as well.

The doctor said, "Sometimes a baby's system doesn't accept the vaccinations we give them. It rarely happens, but I am pretty sure that's what happened this time. There's no way of predicting the reaction. Sometimes the effects are short term and the baby is fine in a couple of days. Sometimes, the effects are more severe and more permanent."

J. P. stood absolutely still, his heart pounding. Laura Dell looked around the little room as if it was a prison cell.

"Long term effects," the doctor continued, "sometimes include mild to severe cases of autism."

J. P. sat down and put his arms around Laura Dell and they whispered together, "No, no, no, no." But, they knew, and the doctor knew that "no" was probably not the right answer this time.

"I'll schedule some tests for next week to see what path we need to take. If anything changes, even a slight amount, I want you to bring him in. We'll give you a call by the end of the week. Other than that, it's just wait and hope and pray. And I mean pray. Get everyone you know to pray." The doctor stood up and turned to go out of the door. Laura Dell heard him sniff and saw him wipe his eyes as he disappeared around the corner.

At home, J. P. sat on the couch with his son on his lap. Laura Dell asked, "Are you going back to work?"

"No, not today. I'll call them and tell them that I will be in tomorrow". He shook his head and looked away.

"I'll fix some lunch," Laura Dell said. She needed to find something for her hands to be doing, something for her mind to be thinking. A terrible change had struck them. It would affect everything about their lives.

Chapter Five

DOCTOR WILLIAMS CALLED A FEW days later. He would have a specialist in his office Monday at nine o'clock. He said that this doctor had dealt with many cases like theirs and she would bring some information with her.

The doctor's name was Carla Padgett. She had Michael Angelo's file on a desk when the Higgins family came in to see her. She took Michael Angelo into her lap and looked into his eyes. She spoke quietly to him as she listened to his heart and lungs and did all of the other routine checks. "He seems to be quite healthy. Has there been any diarrhea or vomiting?"

"No, he's been normal physically," Laura Dell answered. "He's not active like he's supposed to be. He doesn't seem to recognize us or respond to us at all. He's so quiet. He was a bundle of noise and action before he got those shots."

"Was he talking at all before... was he talking last week?" Doctor Padgett asked. "Did he understand words like "eat" and "go"? Could he say "Momma and Daddy?"

"He said Momma and Papa. He calls J. P. Papa. And he would say, 'Bye', and throw a kiss."

"Has he tried to communicate with you at all since this happened?" The doctor looked at his ears and held her palm against his temple.

"No. He will open his mouth to eat and drink, but that's all."

Doctor Padgett handed Michael Angelo over to his mother. "I have my equipment in the room here. I want you to hold him while I attach some sensors to his head. It's not painful or uncomfortable for him, so he'll be fine. This takes about three minutes. All you have to do is sit and hold him."

The test made no noise at all, only a few lights blinked on and off on the equipment. After the test was over, the doctor said that she would call them at home when she had analyzed the results. She handed J. P. a large stack of books and pamphlets. "There's a lot of information here. I recommend that both of you begin reading it immediately. The books are numbered, like one, two, three. That's how you should read them. Keep a pen or highlighter with you and mark sections that you have questions on or that you might need to come back and review."

Laura Dell asked, "How much different will this be from the way we have been taking care of him?"

The doctor said, "I don't know." And then she said, "Let me add something. I need to look at the test results, but I am going to take a guess, and it's just a guess, mind you. From what I see today, Michael Angelo is not a worst case scenario child. I think he will be able to communicate and maybe eventually learn to read and write to some extent. But exactly how much he can develop mentally and socially is not predictable. It never is. This baby is still a person and he is going to grow and develop in complicated ways with a nature that is his alone. So you will adjust to who he is, and as time goes by, he will adjust to who you all are. You should begin to focus immediately on communication. The first book will help you with that. I'll be available whenever you need me. Michael Angelo is my patient now. No matter what, don't give up on him. He has a life of his own to live. Let's help him have a good one."

Laura Dell and J. P. both said, "Thank you, Doctor."

Laura Dell sat quiet and still as J. P. drove them home. There was a calmness about her, a building strength. She said, "That doctor seems to be dedicated to her work. I think I am going to like her."

J. P. said, "Yeah, I hope the books are as plain spoken and understandable as she is. Let's do like she said and study them, but I think we should trust our instincts as well. I don't plan to follow a doctor's advice if I have a bad feeling about it ever again."

"That makes sense," Laura Dell said, looking at her husband, an intense expression on her face. "Let's always ask questions, no matter how small they seem to be. Let's ask, and let's get straight answers from now on. That was one of the things I liked about Doctor Padgett. When she answered our first question, she said she didn't know. Then she gave us her best guess. She gave us a general answer with a lot of room to figure things out for ourselves. That's a better doctor, I think, than one who is inflexible."

When they made it into the house, Michael Angelo was asleep, so Laura Dell put him to bed and immediately grabbed the top book, numbered "one", and sat down on the couch.

J. P. went into the kitchen and called back to her, "Do you want a sandwich and a glass of tea?"

"Turkey and cheese with mayonnaise," she answered, only looking up for a second.

The book was well written, the language plain, and there were pictures and diagrams. Communication is the key, it said.

Laura Dell read two chapters, until her eyes were burning and all of the information was beginning to jumble up in her mind. As soon as she laid the book down, J. P. picked it up and started reading.

Laura Dell curled up and put her feet in his lap, "What a sad, sad day," she mumbled. Within a minute, she was asleep.

J. P. would read a few paragraphs, look around the room, and read some more. "Uh huh", he would whisper. "Okay, so.." And then he might write a note to himself or underline a sentence. At the end of the first chapter, he wrote, "Keep talking to him." At the end of the second chapter, he wrote "Repetition." At the end of the third chapter, he wrote, "Order."

When he was too tired to continue reading, he closed the book and set it on an end table. Suddenly, he picked it back up and opened it to the end of the last chapter that he had read. In large capital letters, he wrote "MUSIC" and "EXERCISE."

Hot tears welled up in his eyes. "I know who my baby already is," he whispered. "I know what he likes the most."

Chapter Six

ALL OF THAT WEEK, THE two parents changed almost everything about their home. There was a minimum of everything but open space. All of the furniture was put in a certain place. Toys of solid colors were kept available, but multi-colored items were put away. Basic shapes were preferred; circles, squares, and triangles, balls, cubes, and cones.

Above the mantle in the living room, only three pictures were placed. There was a picture of Laura Dell, of J. P., and of Michael Angelo.

J. P. said, "I know it's going to be nerve wracking for you, but we need to see if this works, and it's going to take some time."

Laura Dell laughed. "It may drive me crazy. This is going to be like that movie, Groundhog Day, only not much will change, and time really will be going by. But if it helps Michael Angelo, it will be worth it."

They wanted repetition. They wanted a daily routine. Their goal was to make almost exactly the same thing happen every day until Michael Angelo began to anticipate what would happen next. There was no way of knowing if he had retained any memory of his life before he became autistic, so they needed to create an instant memory as a foundation from which Michael Angelo's personality would grow.

Every morning at six o'clock, J. P. got ready for work. At six thirty, Laura Dell got Michael Angelo up and dressed him in clothes that she had laid out the night before. Every morning, she sang to him, "Wake up, baby Angelo, there's places that you need to go. Every day's a happy day with things to learn and games to playyyy!" And then, she would always pop him up into her arms and point to the door and say in a cheerful voice, "Let's go!"

The little three-person family would eat a quiet, quick breakfast and J. P. would kiss his wife and his baby good bye and head off to work. Laura Dell would carry Michael Angelo into the living room and stand before the three pictures and say, "Do you know who these people are?" She would point to her picture and say, "This is Momma." Then she would point to J. P.'s picture and say, "This is Papa." And then she would point to Michael Angelo's picture and say, "This is Michael Angelo. This is you."

Over and over, at least four times every morning, she would do this. After the first time, she would take her baby's hand and place the palm on the picture and tell him who each picture was.

After that, Laura Dell would put him in his playpen with a ball, a square block, and a pyramid shaped plastic block. She would hold the ball up and show it to him and say, "This is a ball." and she would place it in his hand. After a few minutes, she would come back and pick up the block and show it to him and say, "This is a block." And she would place the block in his hand. Then, after a few more minutes, she would do the same with the pyramid. She would finish by placing all three pieces in front of Michael Angelo and putting a small box in the playpen. "Now, you decide which ones you want to put in this box," she would say, and she would show him what she meant by putting the pieces in the box and then putting them all back in front of him.

Whether Michael Angelo played with the toys or not, Laura Dell went about her morning business for a couple of hours. Then she would take the block and the pyramid out and put a toy car and a truck in the playpen. "A car," she would say, "and look, oooh, it's a truck." She would roll them around for a few seconds. The ball always stayed in the playpen with the baby. Laura Dell was hoping for a day when she would be in another room and she would hear a crash and she would rush into the living room only to find that Michael Angelo had thrown the ball across the room and knocked something off of the wall. She didn't care what he broke. She just wanted him to make something make a noise.

After lunch, which was always at eleven thirty, Laura Dell would take the baby out in the yard if the weather was good and they would walk around together. She would show him things: flowers, and trees, and the lawnmower, and drain spouts. She would explain to him what each thing was and what it did and how it worked. They walked around for at least an hour every day. After that, it was time for his nap, and she would lay him in his bed and turn on some soft music and he would sleep for about an hour.

Laura Dell did this, always hoping that Michael Angelo would give her a sign, any sign, that he was self aware. She needed desperately to know that he was in there somewhere trying to find his way back to her. At first, she knew he was. Then, after six months, with no sign that he was noticing anything, she thought he was. Three months later, she hoped he was still in there somewhere. And after three months more, she prayed that her baby was still in there trying to find his way out.

It was after Michael Angelo's second birthday that Laura Dell's hope began to fade. She would sit beside his bed while he took his afternoon nap and cry and pray that her baby would do something different, something to break the repetitive routine. But he never did.

One hot August afternoon when Laura Dell was vacuuming the bedroom, the vacuum cleaner made a popping noise and stopped working. Now, the quietest places in the world, the places where a person can plan, or daydream, or remember are where a person is holding onto a handle. It can be a lawnmower, or a vacuum cleaner, or anything that makes a constant sound. So, when the vacuum quit, it was a serious interruption to Laura Dell.

She set it on the bed and tried to see what had happened to it. A couple of pieces fell out of the bottom. She sat down on the bed beside it.

"Well," she said, as tears welled up into her eyes. "It's not going to work anymore." Her own words echoed back to her in the silent room. "It's not going to work." The words chopped their way into her heart like a dull ax. "It's not going to work," she whispered. She sat slumped over and sobbed. The search for the mind of her son had worn her out. He wasn't in there. He wasn't anywhere. He was gone forever.

That's where she was when J. P. came home from work. When he came into the living room, Michael Angelo was sitting in his playpen. He could see Laura Dell through the bedroom door. She stood up and looked around like she had lost something.

"What's wrong, Laura?" J. P. asked. He could tell that something had happened.

"Let's see, besides the fact that the vacuum cleaner broke, and I'm trapped here in this little bitty house, and now it's late, and I haven't even started supper, and nothing's working like it's supposed to..." She put her hands over her face and began to sob.

J. P. stepped over and put his arms around her and tried to comfort her. "We'll go in the morning and buy you a brand new vacuum." He reached over and turned the radio on.

"We don't have the money," she said, her voice cracking.

"Then, I'll sell the work truck and I'll buy you a brand new expensive vacuum."

She put her arms around her husband. "You silly, it's a company truck".

"Okay", he said, "they can keep the vacuum at the shop when you're not using it."

"Face the truth, J. P. You're dreaming."

At that exact moment, the Oak Ridge Boys song, Dream On, began to play on the radio. J. P. waltzed her into the living room where Michael Angelo was standing in his playpen.

As they danced by him, his eyes followed them and ever so slowly, their little silent son raised his left hand and just above a whisper, he said, "Bapa?"

J. P. swooped him up in one arm, and with his other arm, he embraced his wife who wrapped her other arm around Michael Angelo. They danced around the living room.

Michael Angelo laid his arm across his Papa's shoulder and faced the direction they were going as they danced. Laura Dell whispered, "Oh, thank you, Jesus. Thank you, Jesus." J. P. couldn't say anything. He just danced the whole wad of them around as The Oak Ridge Boys sang.

"Dream on. Dream about the world we're gonna live in one fine day."

Finally. Finally, after more than a year of silence, there was a reason to dream for this family again.

Chapter Seven

THE FACT THAT MICHAEL ANGELO had spoken was an encouragement to Laura Dell, but she was still mentally exhausted. After that three minute dance, her baby was still silent. The sudden miracle was gone like the blink of a faraway beacon, and it didn't blink again to offer guidance.

Something good had happened. Her child had let them know that he was still there. Still, she didn't know what was helping, what was hurtful, and what didn't make any difference at all. Since she had reached the point of exhaustion, Laura Dell was going through the motions of their daily routine without noticing any changes. For a few days, she had hoped desperately that she would see more signs of progress. Every day of every week seemed to be the same. The only thing that changed was that Michael Angelo grew as a child is supposed to grow, physically.

Thanksgiving came and they went to visit their families. The abundance of faces and voices seemed to irritate Michael Angelo. He didn't like unfamiliar surroundings and he spent much of Thanksgiving Day with his eyes closed and with his hands over his ears. This caused the concerned family members to offer suggestions. Too many of the holiday conversations started with, "Have you tried?" or "Maybe you should."

The day after, breakfast was a silent, sad meal. J. P. ate very little. Neither did Laura Dell. Michael Angelo was his usual mechanical self again.

J. P. mumbled, "Well, at least he reacted to something, even if it was to try to block everything out."

Laura Dell stood up. "Shut up, J. P. You don't know what it's like."

"Yes, I do."

Laura Dell started putting the breakfast dishes in the sink. "You're not here all day, everyday, doing the same thing over and over, hoping that something will work, but knowing that time is going by, and he's just.... he's just....."

J. P. said, "But, I am here, Sweetheart."

"No, you're not. I'm by myself. I'm all by myself."

"I promise you. You're not by yourself. I'm with you. Don't give up. Please don't give up. He's going to wake up."

They didn't look at each other, but neither one of them walked out, either. The intensity of their emotions at the moment could not make a crack in their love for each other. J. P. stayed in his chair. Somehow, he knew this was not a time for touching each other. Laura Dell was fighting a battle inside of her soul, a battle that had been going on for a long, long time. Finally, Laura Dell said, "We are going to have to try something else. The books are helpful, but if Michael Angelo is as tired of this routine as I am, it's no wonder he isn't reacting. He's bored. He can't tell one day from the next, and neither can I."

J. P. said, "Alright then, let's do the opposite. Let's change everything. We can even do it at night. Let's change everything around while he's asleep. There's only two things that I think he has to have. He has to be able to see us, and he has to have music."

"Music?" Laura Dell snapped. "I was thinking you would say he needed a ball." Then, she smiled. "I think he needs a ball. It's me. I think he needs one."

"He needs a dozen!" J. P. said.

That night, they moved furniture. They took most of the balls that were stored away out of the toy box and put them in Michael Angelo's playpen. They covered the bottom of the playpen with toys. When Michael Angelo woke up on Saturday morning, J. P. dressed him. He put a nice warm jacket on him and instead of going straight to breakfast, they went outside. Instead of walking around in the yard, J. P. took him for a walk down the road.

When Michael Angelo seemed to be getting tired of walking, J. P. picked him up. He talked constantly to his son, "Don't give up, baby. Life lasts a long time and you're only a little behind. You'll catch up in a little bit.

All you have to do is get started. Momma is waiting for you to talk to her so you can tell her that you love her. When you start talking, you can tell her about this time. You can tell her how her love was your strength. You'll find your way. I know you will."

They ate their breakfast that morning with the kitchen door open. A cool breeze blew through, bringing the sounds of the outside world. After they had finished, Laura Dell carried Michael Angelo into the living room. Out of habit, she stopped and asked him, "Do you know who this is?" She pointed to the picture of herself. "This is Momma."

Not breaking her routine, she asked who each picture was. When she started the second pass through the pictures, instead of waiting for her to lift his hand, Michael Angelo put the palm of his hand on her picture. Her voice trembling, she said, "This is Momma. Now, where's Papa?"

As she moved over half a step, her baby put his hand on J. P.'s picture. She took another short step. She waited to see if he would touch the picture before she spoke his name. He did not move! "Where's your picture?" she whispered. "Where's Michael Angelo?"

Michael Angelo placed his little palm on his own picture and turned to face his mother, a half-smile on his lips. His eyes were bright and focused!

"Oh, my sweet baby!" she cried. "Oh, my little lost Michael Angelo! J. P.! Come here, I want to show you something."

J. P. came into the room. Laura Dell said, "Michael Angelo, where's Papa?"

At first, the baby didn't move, but he had such a look on his face. It was mischief. He was teasing them. "Where's Papa?" Laura Dell asked him again.

Michael Angelo leaned out, and with the palm of his hand, patted the picture of J. P. one, two, three, four times.

There was no doubt! He understood. This picture is Momma. And this picture is Papa. And this picture is me. I am Michael Angelo!

Chapter Eight

NOW, THERE WAS A CHANGE. Laura Dell knew two things for sure. Michael Angelo understood what she was saying and he was capable of speech. So, communication with her son had been established. Also, the breakthrough had come after a morning walk before breakfast.

On Monday morning, she let him sleep until he woke up on his own. She laid his clothes on a low table and asked him what he wanted to put on first. Even though he didn't point or try to speak, she noticed that he looked at his shirt. So, she put his shirt on him. After she put his pants on, she asked, "Michael Angelo, where are your shoes?" She put him on the floor and asked again, "Where are your shoes?" They were beside his feet, but he didn't look at them or look for them.

"Oh, well," she said. "Little by little." After she had slipped his shoes on his feet, she started into the living room, watching to see if he would follow her. When he didn't, she turned around and took his hand, but he resisted. When she tried to pick him up, he pulled away and screamed at her; no words, just a scream. "What is it?" She reached for him again, but he stepped away from her. She looked into his eyes to see if he was in pain, but that didn't seem to be the problem.

The only expression she could detect was that his bottom lip was pooched out a little. Although she was concerned, she gave a quick laugh. "Michael Angelo, are you pouting? Did Momma hurt your feelings?" She looked around and wondered at the same time. "What could I have done that he thinks is wrong?" she asked herself, speaking out loud. He was dressed. They always left the bedroom after he was dressed in the morning. She reached for him again. Again he stepped away, almost panicking.

Laura Dell's mind was racing, "What should I do? Should I grab him and force him to come with me? No, I don't want to do that." She sat on the bed, but jumped right back up. Today was not the day for a setback. She wasn't going to allow it.

"Hey, I know what I can try! Wake up, baby Angelo, there's places that you need to go. Every day's a happy day with things to learn and games to playyyy!"

She reached for his hand and he didn't resist this time. Smiling at his face, she pulled him up to land on her hip and then up a little higher. "Let's go!" she said, and he laid his arm across her shoulder as they marched out of the bedroom.

That was the morning Laura Dell learned that Michael Angelo felt very strongly about starting every day with a song and she was supposed to sing it. It did help. In the days and months to come, no matter how the day before had ended, the next morning would always start with a song. There is something about a song that energizes a person.

So, some habits were kept. Some were discarded. Laura Dell moved the three pictures down close to eye level for Michael Angelo so he could look directly at them and touch them if he wanted to. As he grew, he climbed into and out of his playpen as he pleased. This became his first method of self determined activity. He would climb into the playpen and toss everything out of it and then climb out and toss it all back in. This activity grew in width and length as he became more confident. The balls bounced and rolled all over the room. Somehow, he knew exactly how many toys were in the room and he didn't stop gathering them until every one of them was tossed back into the playpen. After a few months, he was throwing balls from across the room and landing them in the playpen with regularity.

Laura Dell was amused at the game he had made up for himself and she was glad that he had started throwing balls around again. But her efforts to get him to speak seemed to be failing. He would point at things. He would look at something if he wanted it. He would come and stand in front of her until she figured out what he wanted. She knew that he had a good sense of time, because he would often go and stand patiently in the kitchen and wait for his Papa to come through the door and pick him up and dance him around the room. But so far, he didn't seem to be interested in speaking.

One morning, she was in the bed room straightening things up when she thought she heard somebody talking. It sounded like they were outside, so she started for the door, but the voice wasn't outside. It was the voice of Michael Angelo. He was standing in front of the three pictures. He touched Laura Dell's picture and said, "This Momba." Then he stepped over and touched J. P.'s picture and said, "This Bapa." And he stepped again, looked at his own likeness and said, "This me. This me. Me Angel." he pronounced his name with the "A" sounding like it does in Angelo.

Laura Dell didn't interrupt her son. She stood still as he taught himself, and it occurred to her that he may have been secretly trying out things as he learned them all along. She decided that their most likely hope for success in teaching him was to show him how something is done several times and then tell him to do it. She would give him time alone so he could figure out his own way.

When he stopped talking to the pictures, he looked up and saw her watching him. With a half smile on his face, he said, "Momba, me Angel."

Laura Dell smiled at her son and said, "Yes, you certainly are."

Chapter Nine

LAURA DELL CALLED DOCTOR PADGETT and told her how Michael Angelo had secretly taught himself to speak in short sentences. The doctor said, "I think you should increase the mental challenges. Give him puzzles. Add more interactive toys, both inside and outside. Also, he might be ready to increase his social skills."

Laura Dell said, "I don't know about that. He seems to go backwards when there are more people around. Too many people talking at one time, or too many strangers talking to him at once causes him to freak out."

"Well, do you think that next year he's going to have an easier time adjusting to society? Will he automatically mature if he isn't exposed to other people, people that he doesn't know? How will he make friends if he never meets somebody new?"

Laura Dell said, "Well, uh, I don't know. It's hard for him to be around strangers."

Doctor Padgett said, "Of course it is. He's autistic. But he's also a person. He will be afraid. He will do some intense acting to let you know that he's afraid. Sometimes, it's going to break your heart when he is screaming and kicking and fighting because he thinks that he wants to be left alone. But to keep him hidden from the world would be the most abusive, barbaric thing you could do to him."

Laura Dell asked, "How do I start out? Do I ease him into social situations, or do I take him to daycare tomorrow and go back to my job?"

Doctor Padgett said, "Let's try interactive television, cartoons and stuff like that. Take him with you when you go to the grocery store and the hair dresser. Take him everywhere you go and introduce him to everybody. Fill his life with new faces. If he pitches a fit, don't make a big deal out of it. Don't be too forceful with him, because he will probably act worse if you do."

"Okay, I'll give it a try."

"Laura Dell," the doctor said, "I expect you to do more than try. I expect you to excel at being Michael Angelo's mother and his guide through a meaningful and productive life. He is here for a reason. None of us know what that reason is. Let's find out. And let's be glad when we do find out."

Laura Dell thanked the doctor and put down the phone. "Oh, Lord," she said. "Well, here we go. Let's see."

The television was left turned on all day except during nap time. The radio was playing music during his naps.

Laura Dell bought some simple puzzles that Michael Angelo could put together. She showed him how they worked. At first, he liked doing them, but after a few months, he had mastered each one.

He would watch the television for a few minutes and lose interest. There were some shows that did hold his attention. If the show had a group of children and they were singing and dancing, he would try to dance along with them, but his command of language was far behind the shows, so he became frustrated with singing.

There was a cartoon that he loved. It was Casper, the Friendly Ghost. Laura Dell ordered a set of tapes that was all Casper. Michael Angelo would stand in front of the television and watch, sometimes talking in short words to the ghosts and Wendy, the little witch who was Casper's friend. Several times, Laura Dell heard Michael Angelo say, "Casper, me Angel," and "Wendy, me Angel."

Laura Dell started taking Michael Angelo with her more often when she went to town. She let him walk along beside her instead of riding in the shopping cart. At first he didn't like it because he was unsure about walking through a big store. He tried to get into the cart, but Laura Dell insisted that he walk.

There was a breakthrough for Michael Angelo when, in the children's clothes department one day, he saw some pajamas that had pictures of Casper and Wendy on them.

"Momma," he said, his eyes big and excited, "This Casper. This Wendy."

"Do you want these for your pajamas?" Laura Dell held them out for Michael Angelo to feel.

"Me wear now, Momma."

Laura Dell put them in the shopping cart. "No, you'll have to wait until tonight. They're pajamas. You can wear them tonight when you go to bed."

"Me wear now. Angel wear now." He tried to take them out of the cart.

Laura Dell put her hand on the pajamas and held them firmly in place. "Wait until we get home, and then you can put them on."

"Angel wear now, Momma. Give it."

"No, son. I have to pay for them and you have to wait until we get home."

Michael Angelo began to try to climb up on the side of the cart and pull the pajamas out, but Laura Dell held them firmly. He started screaming and snatching at anything he could get a hold of in the cart. Laura Dell calmly took whatever he picked up away from him and put it back in the cart.

"Angel want it now!" He sat down in the floor and folded his arms across his chest.

Laura Dell almost laughed. "Boy, you better get up out of that floor."

While she was discussing the action that her son needed to take, a lady who had been observing Michael Angelo's behavior dropped a tee shirt in Laura Dell's cart. It had "I'm a little Angel" printed on the front and a picture of a little boy with a halo above his head, but a mischievous look on his face. Laura Dell didn't notice what had happened.

Michael Angelo refused to get up and walk, so she picked him up and put him in the seat of the shopping cart and let him hold the pajamas. This ended the argument until it was time to check out. Michael Angelo didn't want to let go of the pajamas long enough to let the cashier ring them up.

The struggle over who would hold the Casper pajamas didn't last long. Laura Dell won. But the fit that Michael Angelo pitched lasted all the way to the car, and even after he was safely buckled into his seat and had the pajamas in his hands, he was still screaming.

Laura Dell didn't notice the tee shirt until she was home. Michael Angelo was demanding that she put the Casper pajamas on him right now. She said, "Okay, let me get them unwrapped. Good night, son! You need to calm down or you're not going to get to watch any Casper today."

"Angel wear Casper jambers now!"

"Okay, you start taking your pants and shirt off while I get your Caspers open."

"Okay, Momma," and Michael Angelo began trying to pull his shirt off, but he couldn't get it over his head. Then he tried to pull his pants off, but he couldn't get them over his shoes. He expressed his frustration with grunts and groans and finally screams and tears.

It was while Laura Dell was watching Michael Angelo and unfolding the pajamas that she discovered the Angel shirt. "I didn't buy this. Did I buy this?" She sorted through the bags and looked at her receipt. "Oops. I bought it." She looked at the shirt, and then she looked at her son. "Ohhh, you shouldn't have pitched that fit."

Laura Dell helped Michael Angelo get his pants and shirt off. Then she put the pajama bottoms on him. He stood up and put his hands on his belly and looked down at them with satisfaction. "Casper pants," he said. "Put shirt on."

"Here you go," Laura Dell said with a smile. And then she put the "I'm a little Angel" shirt on Michael Angelo.

Michael Angelo looked down and saw that he wasn't wearing a Casper shirt. He tried to pull the "Angel" shirt off, but he couldn't. "Momma, take off."

"No. Do you know what it says?"

"Not say Casper. Take off."

"Don't you want to know what it says?"

"Not say Casper. Take off."

Laura Dell didn't move. Michael Angelo didn't have another fit in him. He looked at the shirt for a few seconds and looked at his mother. "What it say, Momma?"

"It says Angel."

Michael Angelo stood there looking at the picture on the shirt. He whispered, "Angel. Me Angel, Momma, me Angel!"

"That's right. You're Angel. It's a shirt with your name on it."

He spun around in a circle, looking at his shirt and his pajama pants. "Casper pants and Angel shirt. Casper and Wendy and Angel."

Laura Dell never found out how the Angel shirt wound up in her shopping cart. She never knew that somebody thought it was a good joke to put it in her groceries because her son was being such a little brat in the store. But the humor wasn't lost, because it was on that day, when Michael Angelo had behaved so badly, that his name became Angel. It said so on his shirt.

Chapter Ten

THE MONTHS HAD FLOWN BY. Angel's mental growth had suffered such a severe setback that Laura Dell and J. P. decided there was no hope of putting him in kindergarten when he was five years old. He was completely unable to read. He hardly knew how to count and he had a minimal understanding of colors.

On his fifth birthday, they gave him learning materials and a bicycle. He had pencils and crayons and coloring books and writing pads and a bicycle. He also had large plastic pieces that snapped together which were shaped like numbers and letters so he could create words and numbers. And, of course, he got a kick ball with large numbers on it.

That Spring, it was hard for Laura Dell to keep Angel inside. He wanted to ride his bicycle. After three weeks, she took the training wheels off, and Angel wore a trail in the grass around the edge of the yard, riding and riding and riding. If the weather was sunny, which it usually was, he refused to come inside until he was very tired. Then, of course, he wanted to take his nap. He was too tired to learn about numbers and letters.

After a nap, he was full of energy again and he wanted to ride his bicycle. Time went by. He rode his bicycle. He learned very little. He was locked into the circle around the yard and Laura Dell didn't know how to get him interested in anything else.

One Saturday afternoon, she was sitting with J. P. on the porch while Angel rode circles around the yard. It was such a beautiful day. She wanted to relax and be warm and comfortable and content with life, but the situation with Angel and the bicycle had to be addressed.

"All he does all day long is ride that bicycle," she said to J. P. "He's not learning anything. He has to learn to read. He needs to learn how to interact with other children. Learning anything doesn't come easy for him. I don't know what to do. If I take away his bicycle, he's going to fight like crazy to get it back."

J. P. shook his head and said, "I know. I have been tumbling it over in my head for a while. There must be some way of letting him know that he needs to learn other things. He wants to stay on that bicycle. He doesn't sense time. Everything is now, and now is when he should ride his bicycle."

Laura Dell asked, "Do you have any ideas about how to get him off of it?"

"I don't have a one. If we take it away from him for half of a day so he can learn, he will probably pitch a fit and refuse to do anything. I wonder what we can do to make him want to learn instead of riding his bicycle."

They sat together, wondering. Laura Dell said, "We will have to make riding his bicycle a privilege or a reward. And it will have to be everyday, too."

J. P. said, "Yeah, and it won't be easy. He already has that privilege." All of a sudden, he jumped to his feet. "I think I have an idea. And I will be the bad guy, so Angel doesn't argue with you all day about the bicycle."

Laura Dell said, "Let me hear that idea, then. I am dreading the arguments about the bicycle more than anything else."

On Monday morning, after the family had eaten breakfast, J. P. said, "Momma, have you written your A B C's yet?"

Laura Dell said, "No, Papa, I have not."

"Well, have you written your numbers from one to ten yet?"

"No, Papa, I have not."

"Have you learned your colors yet?"

"No, Papa, I have not."

J. P. yelled, "Why not?" and banged the kitchen table with his fist.

Laura Dell and Angel both jumped at the sound. She said, "Because, I have been outside with Angel while he rides his bicycle."

J. P. put as angry of an expression as he could make on his face and said, "Momma, you and Angel have to stay in until after lunch every day until you learn to write and count and tell your colors. And Angel, you have to teach her."

Angel was afraid to say anything.

J. P. kissed them both and left for work.

Laura Dell said, "Angel, now Papa is mad at us. I have to learn to write and count and tell all of the colors. Will you help me?"

Angel smiled and said, "Momma, me help you."

"You will?"

"Yeah, Angel help Momma. How I help?"

Laura Dell started teaching Angel that day. They would go over the letters first, and then the numbers, and finally the colors. After lunch, if Angel was still interested in letters, the lessons would continue. If not, Angel was allowed to ride his bicycle. Within a week, he was counting how many times he had ridden around the yard, and Laura Dell made cards so he could see the numbers.

The lessons continued with letters and colors as well. Each time he would ride by, Laura Dell would ask, "What color is this, Angel?"

"Green! Green means go!"

"How many times around?"

"Five! Me five years old!"

All through the summer afternoons, the boy on the bicycle rode around and learned. By September, he could make the sounds of each letter. He could write his name and Momma and Papa and Casper and Wendy. He would help Laura Dell write notes to J. P., telling him that she was learning a lot and trying very hard. She would tell him what to write and help him spell the words. He was never allowed to leave a word spelled incorrectly, because they didn't want Papa to get upset.

This was wonderful progress. Laura Dell and J. P. were so proud of Angel. One night, after Angel had gone to sleep, Laura Dell said, "I think he may be able to go to school. Maybe not this year, but next fall, he should be ready to start in the first grade. He is already past what some kids know when they start kindergarten."

J. P. said, "You have done such a good job with him. You're the best Momma in the whole world. That's why I didn't tell you that I got a promotion at the first of the year, because you're so good, and I love you so much."

Laura Dell asked, "How did you get a promotion? Your check hasn't gone up."

"They held back my raise for a year. I will get it all as back pay in January. That way taxes won't eat it up, see."

Laura Dell didn't know whether to be mad or not. Her mind was racing. Her heart was pounding. There were so many things that they needed. "How....how big was the raise?"

J. P. smiled. "Guess."

"Ten thousand."

"Higher."

" How much higher, fifteen thousand?"

"Higher."

"No way."

J. P. smiled; actually, he grinned. "Twenty five thousand dollars!"

Tears came into Laura Dell's eyes. She had been burdened with sadness because they had so little, and she couldn't go back to work because Angel needed special attention. J. P. never complained. He worked, sometimes too many hours, and there was never enough money to do anything special. There were no vacations or fishing trips. For five years, it was all work.

J. P. was still smiling like he had a secret. "That ain't all," he said.

Laura Dell couldn't think of anything else that could be added on to a twenty five thousand dollar raise. "Tell me all, then," she said, a short giggle coming out at the end of her demand.

"You know the owner of the company, Mister Garrett?"

"Yeah."

"Well, he had an elderly uncle that owned a little farmhouse out in the Easy Creek community. You know, that house where the old mill used to be."

Laura Dell said, "Oh, I know which house you're talking about. I love that old house."

"Mister Garrett's uncle owned it, but he died, and none of his kids live around here, so they asked Mister Garrett to see if he could sell it. He asked me if I wanted to buy it. So, one day after work, we went over and looked around, and I said, how much. And he said, for me, forty thousand. And I said, how much land, and he said the original homestead was still intact, so forty acres."

Laura Dell said, "And you said sold! Oh, please tell me you said sold!"

"I said sold! We are going to own our own house, Laura Dell! It's furnished already, and it's got a creek, and a barn, and a big old field for Angel to rip and romp and ride his bike."

Laura Dell didn't care about being left out of the decision to buy the house. She could make a whole bunch of decisions while they were moving and after they had finished moving. She was sure she could be even with J. P. by the time they had settled into their new home.

J. P. said, "There was one big reason that I wanted to move out to Easy Creek. They have a little school out there, Easy Creek Elementary School. When he starts middle school, Angel will go to Cedar Ridge, but for the first five years, he gets to go to school right down the road from the house. To me, that's the best reason to move. Angel gets to start out in a small school where everybody will know him. That's the best part as far as I'm concerned."

They slept well that night. Both of them dreamed of a future with a little more sunshine in it.

Chapter Eleven

DURING THE NEXT FEW MONTHS, Laura Dell and J. P. worked on fixing up the old farmhouse. There were some minor repairs needed, and J. P. decided that all of the wiring should be replaced. Every weekend and many afternoons were spent in the dark cold house.

That winter was a cold winter. Sometimes J. P. would work by himself because Laura Dell didn't want Angel to catch a cold. Almost all of the Christmas money was spent on material for the new house, which was fine with both Laura Dell and J. P.

Angel didn't quite understand the idea of moving to a new home. Every time his parents talked to him about his new home and his new bedroom, he expected to either move that very minute, or to wake up in his new bed-room the next morning. Several times, he started taking his clothes out of the dresser and putting them in boxes or bags, anything he could find to carry them.

Laura Dell would say, "Angel, what are you doing?"

Angel would always give the same answer, "Me moving to my new room by the creek."

"Not yet, son. We still have to get more things done before we move. It's going to be a few days."

"Angel move now. You and Papa come tonight when he gets home from work."

Sometimes there would be an argument. Angel would snatch the clothes out of the drawers as fast as Laura Dell could put them back in. When he thought that a decision had been made, his mind became locked in the moment. They were going to move to the new house. Angel was going to sleep in his new bedroom. That was all that mattered to him. Moving was the next action to be taken. When a child thinks in a straight line, when a statement is as solid as an object, it is difficult for him to understand that planned actions do not happen immediately. He feels trapped, and the only way out of the trap is to do what he was told he was going to do. Sometimes, Angel would argue and struggle until both he and his mother were exhausted.

She tried to remember how his mind worked. She tried to keep her patience, and most of the time she did.

That winter, when it was too cold to go outside, Laura Dell created a game where she would say a short sentence and Angel would snap together letters that spelled the words of the sentence, and then he might use objects in the room to show what the sentence meant.

For instance, she would say, "The ball is blue."

Angel would get a blue ball and put it at the end of the sentence after he snapped the letters together that spelled the words.

"Angel is running." was a favorite because he could make the sentence and then run around the room. With Laura Dell's help, Angel could make sentences with five or six words and fully understand what they meant. To Laura Dell, this was a major step in his ability to understand language. She learned something else as well. Variations in the methods that she used to teach Angel made the lessons seem like games. He was gaining knowledge quickly. She was certain he would be ready for first grade by the next fall.

Finally, in February, the house was ready. One sunny afternoon, with the hint of Spring in the air, J. P. took his little family for a walk around the property.

Forty acres is a pretty good chunk of land. There was the old house, fixed up nicely now, with a pea gravel driveway that came up to the side door which opened into the kitchen. About fifty yards behind the house, at the edge of the big yard, was an old barn. It wasn't ready to fall down yet, but the cost to repair it would have been about the same as what it would take to build a new one. They decided to leave it alone for now and let nature take its course. There had been a fenced in pasture at one time, but now it was gone. All that was left of it was the gate, two large cedar posts and a welded steel pipe frame, flung open years ago and left to rust itself away.

Just past the gate was an ancient apple tree, gnarled and ugly in the gray winter without any leaves to hide the scars the years had left along the branches. There was a rutted set of tracks that led straight away from the gate. Far out, a steep ridge rose up from the field. As they walked along the farm road, J. P. pointed out the smooth running stream that bordered the field. "Do you see that, Angel? That's Easy Creek. When the weather gets warmer, we can go fishing in that creek."

Angel walked to the edge of the creek. "Angel not see any fish. Where fish, Papa?'

"Oh, they go live somewhere else during the winter. They'll come back when the weather gets warmer."

"Where they go live?"

J. P. laughed. "They live in Florida, where it's always warm and sunny."

Angel stood for a few minutes looking into the water before turning away and coming back to walk with his parents.

The little creek was well named. It had a slow, steady flow along the side of the field, and they all walked along at an easy pace themselves. As they approached the steep ridge, the flow of the creek quickened and soon they were looking at smaller streams coming down through the rocks and joining together to make the main creek. Here and there were small waterfalls. At the end of the field, there was a place under a big oak tree where stones had been placed in a circle. Many fires had been built over the years.

Laura Dell looked around, picturing in her mind the trees all covered with green leaves and a cool breeze blowing through them. She held J. P.'s hand and said, "What a beautiful place for a picnic. We won't ever have to go on vacation. We can come out here and spend a whole day. That will be good enough for me."

They walked all around the field and back to the old gate. Where the creek crossed the front edge of the field, there was the ruins of an old mill. Not much was left of it. Time and weather had carried away most of the structure, but the dam had been created by a genius. The banks on each side of the channel were poured concrete about four feet tall. And the bottom of the creek was made of concrete as well for about one hundred feet upstream. The dam itself was a steel plate a solid one inch thick. It was welded to a large round shaft which spanned the creek about three feet above the water. The ends of the shaft were set in short sections of pipe on each side of the creek. Those pipes were mounted on top of the concrete walls which formed the side of the creek.

This allowed the metal plate, which acted as the dam, to swing backwards away from the flowing water. The stronger the current, the farther away the plate could swing. Unless there was a huge flood, the swinging dam could keep the water level of the creek at the same depth, which was about three feet deep. It was never too swift and it was never too deep. It was an easy creek.

Most of their new home was beautiful already, and what wasn't could be made that way.

Chapter Twelve

IN MARCH, THE HIGGINS FAMILY moved to Easy Creek. After living in such a small rental house for so long, their new house felt like a mansion. The living room was huge. The television was set against a wall. Laura Dell and J. P. felt like they were walking into a theater at first. It took several weeks for them to adjust to the abundance of space.

Angel became a running, bouncing explorer of every inch of his new home. He loved the hardwood floors, and the rhythmic thump, thump, thump of his running feet could be heard all hours of the day. A new bicycle track was soon evident. It encircled the whole yard, many times larger than his track around the little yard in town.

One day, while a warm spring rain was falling, Angel was watching his Casper cartoons. Laura Dell could hear him talking to the television as he usually did when Casper and Wendy were playing. She heard his voice get louder for a minute, and then she heard his feet making a steady stepping sound on the floor. Bump, bump, bump. Bump, bump, bump. A few seconds later, she heard the same pattern of sounds again.

She went into the living room to see what her son was up to. At the moment, he was rewinding the tape. Then, he stepped back to watch. Without interrupting, Laura Dell moved closer so she could see the television screen.

Angel was watching the Casper episode in which the older witches make magic shoes for Wendy. When she puts them on, she starts dancing and she can't stop. As soon as the music starts, she starts doing a very simple three step dance; three steps to the right and then three steps to the left. The little cartoon witch can't control her magic shoes and she says, "I can't stop dancing!"

As Laura Dell watched, Angel called back to Wendy, "Me can't stop dancing, too!" He danced across the room, perfectly mimicking the three steps, back and forth. As soon as the dance scene was over, Angel ran to the television and rewound the tape. He waited until the music started and danced along with Wendy.

Wendy couldn't stop dancing and neither could Angel.

Finally, Angel noticed his mother watching him. "Momma, Angel can dance! Me dance with Wendy. Come on, Momma, you dance with us, too. We do Casper dance."

Not wanting to discourage Angel's newly discovered activity, Laura Dell danced. And she couldn't stop dancing. Angel insisted that they dance and dance and dance.

To tell the truth, there was something joyful about the simple little dance, and there was something special, almost spiritual about watching Angel dance. His movements were not jerky like a little seven year old boy's should have been. He was smooth, stepping along exactly and in perfect time with Wendy.

Laura Dell wondered about that. Was she being vain, or could she see an underlying talent in her son? Finally, Angel decided they had danced long enough. He didn't say anything. He just stopped dancing and sat down in the floor and started watching the rest of the cartoon.

Laura Dell was winded from the exercise. After she caught her breath, she asked, "Angel, do you like to dance? I think you're a very good dancer."

Angel looked over his shoulder at her and said, "Angel dance all the time, Momma. Me dance when me asleep. Me dance a lot when me asleep."

Laura Dell's mouth fell open. "Do you mean that you dream about dancing?"

"Yeah, me hear music and me dance around. Me always dancing in my sleep. Angel dance on bicycle. Angel dance and run. But, Momma, when Angel sleep, me dance everywhere."

Laura Dell stood there, looking at the back of her little boy. She had always felt that he was alone and unhappy in there. She knew that the puzzle of life didn't always fit together for him. He could not grasp some of the abstract truths of life. Apparently, he had found joy in music and dancing. Somehow, he understood the connection between them. This made Laura Dell glad. She thought that a light was beginning to shine out of Angel. Maybe there was something special happening for him.

When J. P. came home from work that day, he said, "Oh, Lord I am tired." He plopped down on the couch to rest for a few minutes.

"Oh, no you don't," Laura Dell said, a big smile on her face. "You need to get a drink of water and take a deep breath. You can't fall over just yet." She grabbed J. P.'s wrist and began to pull him up.

"What in the world?" J. P. asked. "Did something break?"

"Nope. Something new happened." Looking over her shoulder, she called, "Angel, turn on the Casper dance. Papa wants to learn the Casper dance."

J. P. laughed, "What's a Casper dance? Is it a ghost dance?"

"No, it's a magic witch dance. You have to have magic shoes, J. P. Wendy has magic shoes!"

Angel had rewound the tape, and the scene began. Laura Dell stood J. P. beside Angel and said, "Do what Wendy does. Angel will show you."

The music started and Angel said, "Me can't stop dancing!" and the dance was on. J. P. caught on quickly. Laura Dell stood back and laughed a laugh of pure enjoyment. When Angel ran to the television to rewind the tape, she took her place beside J. P. She leaned towards him and rolled her beautiful brown eyes and blinked a few times. In her most romantic voice, she whispered, "I can't stop dancing, J. P." And the music started.

They danced a family line dance. J. P. added hand and arm movements. Laura Dell added a few hip moves in there as well. Angel was content to follow Wendy's simple three step dance. After about fifteen minutes, Laura Dell said, "Okay boys, that's enough for now. I have to cook supper."

Before she could walk away, J. P. Grabbed her in a tight hug. "How did you teach him to dance?"

Laura Dell hugged him back, "I didn't teach him. I think, maybe you did. You taught him every day when you came home. No matter how tired you were, no matter how bad things seemed to be, you picked our little baby up and danced."

J. P. felt a lump come into his throat. All he could say was, "Oh."

"He told me that he dances in his dreams, J. P." She smiled and eased away from him. "Only you could have taught him to dance and dream at the same time. Only you."

J. P. walked out the door and sat in a chair on the porch. Laura Dell could see him through the kitchen window. His head was bowed and she could see his shoulders shaking.

Angel came into the kitchen and asked, "Where's my Papa?"

Laura Dell picked Angel up and sat him in his chair beside the table. "He's talking to God right now. Let's leave him alone for a few minutes."

"Okay, Momma. Give me a drink. Angel tired from doing Casper dance."

Chapter Thirteen

LAURA DELL WAS CERTAIN THAT Angel could start school in the fall, so she tried to prepare him in as many ways as she thought was possible. There was a church not far down the road and a little grocery store beside the church. Across the road from the church and the store was Easy Creek Elementary School.

One sunny afternoon, as the school day was ending, Laura Dell asked Angel if he would like to take a walk. He thought that was a good idea, so she took him by the hand and they set out for the school. Her timing was perfect. The last few students were leaving when Laura Dell and Angel came strolling into the main office. Laura Dell introduced herself and Angel and asked to speak to the principal.

A stocky little middle aged lady came out of a small office and said, "I am Sarah Anderson, how may I help you?"

Laura Dell said, "Hello, I am Laura Dell Higgins and this is my son, Michael Angelo Higgins. We just moved into the house up the road by the old mill. Angel here is seven years old. He would like to start to school next year"

Mrs. Anderson smiled at Angel and said, "Well, young man, what grade will you be in next year, second?"

Angel took a small step closer to his mother and didn't say anything. Laura Dell answered for him, "Miss Anderson, Angel has never been to school. I have been teaching him at home. He's uh, he's autistic."

Mrs. Anderson looked at Angel for a few seconds and then she took a deep breath. "Laura Dell, how autistic is he?"

"Physically, he's quite strong. Mentally, he learns more by repetition than by concept. He can count and do basic arithmetic. He knows the alphabet and he can write short sentences. He knows colors and shapes." Laura Dell continued in a quiet voice, "My concern is that he hasn't been in a group setting. He has a study schedule until lunch every day and then he gets to play, but that's with just him and me."

Mrs. Anderson said, "This is such a small school. We don't have a special class. I wonder how he might do if we start him in the first grade. Our first grade teacher is a very loving and patient teacher, plus the students will all be new to each other, and I have noticed that at such an early age, they don't make a big deal out of slight differences."

Laura Dell said, "Oh, please let's try and see how he does. He has to develop some social skills and his doctor has already scolded me about keeping him away from gatherings."

Mrs. Anderson said, "I think we should be able to work something out." She stooped down and asked, "Michael Angelo, do you want to go to school here with some other children?"

Angel looked up at Mrs. Anderson and whispered, "Me Angel."

Mrs. Anderson gasped and straightened up, "Is this a visitation?"

Laura Dell laughed, "No, he goes by the name Angel," she said, smiling. "He hardly ever uses words with more than two syllables, and he speaks in short sentences. He just introduced himself, that's all."

Mrs. Anderson's face had turned red. "Well, he certainly does make a first impression." She spoke to Angel without stooping down, "Do you want to go to school and meet some other children who are the same age as you?"

Angel gave his usual half smile and asked, "Is Casper and Wendy at school?"

"I don't know, but you can make friends with some new children, can't you?"

Angel looked up at his mother, but didn't answer. Laura Dell knew that he was thinking about the idea of meeting other children. He would answer when he figured out what meeting other children meant. It might take him a few days.

When neither Angel nor Laura Dell answered, Mrs. Anderson asked another question, "Since you all have just moved in, have you thought about going to church with us? We have a really good pastor. I teach the young children's Sunday School class, so Angel will be in my class. I would love for y'all to come to our church."

Laura Dell said, "You know what? I think we might start coming to church again. And there's no better way to prepare Angel for interaction with other people than a quiet little church."

Mrs. Anderson said, "Great! And call me Tiny. Everybody else does. I think both you and Angel will enjoy spending Sunday mornings in the Lord's house. Do you think your husband will be interested?"

Laura Dell said, "If I tell J. P. that we are going to church this close to the house, he'll start singing a hymn. He loves church."

Mrs. Anderson said, "J. P.? J. P.'s your husband?"

Laura Dell said, "Yes, he is. Do you know him?"

"Just barely. I have seen him in the store a few times. He talks to everybody, doesn't he?"

Laura Dell smiled and said, "Yes, he does."

After their visit with the principal, Laura Dell asked Angel if he wanted to go to the little grocery store and get a drink. As usual, Angel was agreeable, but she could tell that he was still thinking about the idea of school.

The store was different than the big stores in town. There was a wide variety of items in a much smaller space. The lights were not so bright, giving everything a soft glow. There was a friendly quietness about the place. Laura Dell felt like time had slowed down as she led Angel along the short narrow aisles.

A middle aged man called from behind the counter, "Can I help you find something, Ma'am?"

"We just need a coke."

"All the way to the back; I got snacks up here if you need a some chips or a honey bun."

Laura Dell called back, "Okay, thank you." She was in no hurry. Angel was spinning in circles, walking slowly along and trying to look at everything at once.

He said, "Momma, this is store?"

"Yes, this is what people call a country store."

"Why country store?"

"Because it's out in the country, away from town."

Angel held his mother's hand. He snuggled up against her and said, "Stuff might fall."

Laura Dell found the cooler and grabbed a couple of cokes. When she came to the counter, the man took her money and spoke to Angel. "Hello, young man, I'm Mister Green. What's your name?"

Angel said, "Me Angel." Then, he pointed back at the aisles and said, "Stuff might fall."

Mr. Green almost choked, but he laughed instead. "You're right. My son used to help me, but he's in the Marines now, so I don't keep things as straight as I should. How about, in a few years when you get a little bigger, you come to work for me and we'll straighten everything up?"

Angel said, "Angel not fix it. Momma fix it."

Mr. Green laughed out loud.

Laura Dell said, "We just moved here a few months ago, down by the old mill."

Mr. Green's eyes widened, "Ohhh, you're J. P.'s wife!"

"Yes, I'm Laura Dell and this is our son, Angel."

"I am glad to know you both. Y'all need to take a walk every chance you get. Come to the store and get that boy a coke. If something falls on him, I promise I'll help you dig him out."

Laura Dell said, "We might do that," and she opened the door for Angel to go out.

Mr. Green said, "Tell J. P. I hollered at him."

Laura Dell and Angel walked along the shady road. She thought they had been on a very eventful trip. She had met the principal and the Sunday School teacher, and she had found a quiet little store, which Angel thought needed to be straightened up.

Angel had met two new people and talked to both of them.

Chapter Fourteen

ANGEL DID WELL IN SUNDAY School. There were only six or seven children in the class and some of them were naturally quiet. Laura Dell sat in the class with the children as Miss Tiny taught Bible lessons.

There was a difficulty of understanding for Angel. He didn't completely grasp the concept of time. He thought the stories from the Bible had just happened or were happening at that very moment.

One of the teachings that confused him was the act of giving your life to Jesus so you would go to Heaven. Angel thought the trip to Heaven would happen immediately. An idea that couldn't be explained by showing a physical example seemed to be blocked from his limited ability to understand. He understood in a different way, so some stories and examples didn't have the effect they should have. He liked Miss Tiny, though and he liked to hear the new stories she told.

Laura Dell, seeing some of his limitations for the first time in a classroom setting, decided to do all she could to prepare him for school. One of the things she wanted to change was the word choices he always used when referring to himself. He said, "Angel" or "me." He never used the word, "I." To Laura Dell, it was baby talk, and she thought it would be a mark against him if he didn't form the habit of saying, "I."

Sometimes, autism manifests itself in dramatic ways. Angel was a very well behaved child, and even though he learned new things a little slowly, he did eventually learn. But he could not unlearn anything and somehow, in his mind, he had figured out that "me" meant him, Angel, and "I" meant anybody else who was referring to themselves.

Laura Dell didn't know how solidly the word "me" was fastened into Angel's mental collection of words. One day, she sat down in the floor with her son and said, "Angel, who am I?"

"You Momma."

"And who are you?"

"Me Angel, Momma." He smiled a loving little smile.

Laura Dell said, "If I say 'I am Momma', you understand that I am telling you who I am don't you?"

"Momma, Angel knows you."

"Right, so if I say 'I am Momma', then you should say 'I am Angel', okay?"

"No, me Angel. You Momma."

"Yes, but instead of saying 'Me Angel', you should say 'I am Angel.'"

"No, you Momma. Me Angel."

Laura Dell took a breath. "But, you could say, 'I am Angel' and it means the same thing."

"No, me Angel. Me say, 'Me Angel'."

Laura Dell tried another angle. "Papa says, 'I am Papa.' Momma says 'I am Momma', so you should say, 'I am Angel', see?"

"No, me Angel."

"Okay, just say, 'I am Angel' for me. Can you do that?"

"No, me Angel."

"But it means the same thing. If you say, 'Me Angel' or if you say, 'I am Angel', it means the same thing, so I want you to say, 'I am Angel.'"

"No, me Angel. Me not I."

"Yes, you are. When you say, 'I am Angel', you're telling somebody who you are. That's all you're doing."

"No, Momma, me Angel. Me not I Angel. You, I Momma and Papa is I Papa, but me not I Angel. Me Angel, not I."

Laura Dell said, "Listen to me. Me and I mean the same thing. You can say 'me' when you are talking about yourself, and you can say 'I' when you are talking about yourself. Both words mean the same thing."

Angel pointed an angry finger at his mother. "No! Me means Angel! I means Momma!"

Laura Dell felt her patience starting to slip away. "Angel, you can be I, just like Momma and Papa."

"Angel not I! Angel me! Me Angel!" he stood up and turned away from Laura Del, his arms folded across his chest.

"Son, it's not a big deal. I am just trying to teach you how to use a better word when you're talking."

"Angel not I! Angel is Me! Angel is good word. Momma is I. Momma is bad word."

Laura Dell almost laughed. She almost cried at the same time. "Ooh, boy, you better watch how you talk to your Momma."

But, he was already mad. As far as he was concerned, Angel had been insulted. "Me not I! Me not never I. Momma can be I and Papa can be I, but Angel not I! Angel is me! Me Angel, not nobody else, only me Angel!" He started out of the room.

Laura Dell asked, "Where do you think you're going?"

"Angel go outside. Sometimes, you make Papa mad, he go outside. You make Angel mad! You make Angel mad! Me mad at you, Momma. Angel not I! Angel is me!"

He went stomping out through the door. Laura Dell looked out of the window to see where he was. He sat in a chair in the yard with his jaw clenched and his hands in his lap. She didn't know whether to go outside and put her arms around him or to leave him alone until he calmed down. She felt her hands shaking and her heart hurting. "Maybe, in time, he'll understand what I was trying to tell him," she said to herself. "I sure didn't expect that kind of a reaction. Oh, Lord, please help my son do well in school."

After a few minutes, Angel started riding his bicycle around the yard. He didn't seem to be thinking, just riding in circles. Laura Dell hoped that he was rearranging how he understood the words "me" and "I", but there was no way to know if he was or not.

Chapter Fifteen

THE DAYS OF SUMMER FLOW slowly in the country. Laura Dell and Angel would walk to the little store several times a week. Angel developed a half-close friendship with Mr. Green. Angel expected Mr. Green to talk to him and Mr. Green didn't expect any long answers back from Angel, mostly he got stares with an occasional nod. But they did develop the habit of shaking hands every time Angel would leave the store. To Mr. Green, this was a sign of a special companionship.

One morning, as Laura Dell and Angel were leaving their house for a walk to the store, they saw a lady coming down the road pushing a wheelchair.

Laura Dell walked out to the end of the driveway to greet her. She noticed that in the wheelchair was a little girl about Angel's age. The girl had beautiful blonde hair and her skin was so pale that Laura Dell thought she could almost see through it.

"Good morning," Laura Dell said, giving the lady who was pushing the wheelchair a friendly wave.

The lady smiled and stopped, glad to get a quick rest in the shade of a tree. "Whooh! It's getting warm already. Hi! I'm Rachel Daws and this is my daughter, Denise. We call her Neesie."

Laura Dell said, "I'm Laura Dell Higgins and this is my son, Angel. We were heading for the store, is that where y'all are going?"

Rachel said, "It sure is. We can walk along together if you want to."

Laura Dell said, "Of course we can." She motioned for Angel to come along, but he held back a few yards. Laura Dell said, "He's a little shy. He's autistic, and he doesn't meet people very well. It takes a few minutes for him to warm up to a new person."

Rachel said, "I understand. Neesie here is the opposite. She gets started talking and it's hard to turn her off. Maybe they will balance each other out in a little bit. It's best to let nature take its own course, I think."

Laura Dell agreed. The two ladies walked along talking while Angel eased closer and closer to the wheelchair. By the time they made it to the store, Angel was walking along beside Neesie, looking shyly at her, but not saying anything.

Rachel parked the wheelchair next to the counter and walked down the aisle with Laura Dell. Mr. Green said, "Angel, who's your new friend?"

Angel shrugged his shoulders. "Me Angel. Her name Neesie."

Mr. Green smiled at Neesie. "Well, Neesie, it's good to meet you. Any friend of Angel's is a friend of mine."

Neesie looked up at the store owner and said, "I'm not sure we're friends yet. He's kind of quiet, but I guess he's alright."

Mr. Green said, "He's alright, Neesie. Once you get to know him, I'm sure y'all will be buddies."

Angel looked at Mr. Green out of the corner of his eyes and smiled a secret little smile.

The ladies returned with their soft drinks and paid Mr. Green. Laura Dell introduced Rachel and they chatted for a few minutes. Angel gulped his drink down quickly and gave a long, loud burp. He tossed his can into a trash can and shook hands with Mr. Green. He waited outside until the parents and the storekeeper had finished their small talk.

When Laura Dell and Rachel came out of the store, Angel almost mumbled a question. "Angel push Neesie?"

Rachel looked at Laura Dell, an unspoken question in her eyes. Laura Dell gave a quick nod and Rachel said, "Sure, Angel, but if you get tired, let me know and we can take turns, okay?"

Angel said, "Me push," and stepped over and grabbed the push bars. The road was fairly level and the ladies were not in a hurry. Slowing down to keep pace with Angel wasn't a problem. They walked along and talked, getting to know each other.

Rachel lived in the next house past Laura Dell. They had moved in a week ago. Her husband was in the army. He had just been deployed overseas. He expected to be gone for thirteen to fifteen months. Rachel was tired of living on military bases. She was a country girl, and she had never fit in with the lifestyle of close rows of housing and people from all over the nation. The people were friendly, but it was a distant kind of friendly and Rachel didn't adjust well to it.

Laura Dell said, "I'm glad you moved here. I need a few more friends. You can be my newest one."

When they came to Laura Dell and Angel's house, Laura Dell asked Rachel if she wanted to stop and sit for a while. Rachel accepted the offer. They sat in lawn chairs under the shade trees and told each other their stories.

Angel pushed Neesie's chair over by the front porch and sat down next to a post and leaned back. Neesie said, "I won't always be in this wheelchair. I fell out of a swing and hurt my back, but I'm not going to be in it very long. I'm going to walk again."

Angel said, "Angel live here. This my house."

Neesie looked at Angel, but didn't say anything.

For a few minutes, neither one of them spoke. Then, Angel said, "Me go to school in two months."

Neesie said, "I think I will go to the school down by the store. Is that where you go to school?"

Angel said, "Yeah."

"I think that's where I will be going. I'll be in the first grade. I went to kindergarten last year. Did you go to kindergarten? Mommy says first grade is different. She says it's real school. I don't know if I'll like it. Mommy says she will be there the first day, but after that she has to work, so I won't have anybody to push my chair. I don't know what I can do about that. Maybe I'll be walking by then. I hope so. I hope I make new friends. I had a lot of friends before we moved. I don't know anybody here. I like my house, though. We have a fish pond. I like that."

Neesie stopped talking to catch her breath.

Angel said, "Angel push your chair."

"What?"

"Angel push your chair in school."

"Oh!"

"Angel be your friend, too."

"Well, good."

"Angel help you walk again."

"You will?"

"Yeah. Me help Neesie."

Neesie smiled, her eyes as bright as diamonds. "You listened to everything I said, didn't you?"

Angel said, "Yeah. You got fishpond?"

"Oh, yes, and we have koi fish in it. Have you ever seen a koi fish? They look like great big goldfish. The pond is shaped every which a way, like this," and Neesie waved her arms around. "There's a stone walkway that goes all around the pond. Of course, I can't walk right now, but I roll my wheelchair around so I can look at the fish, and there's all kinds of flowers and plants and rocks, big rocks and little bitty rocks. Mommy says it's a garden, but Daddy said it ain't no garden, because you can't pick anything to eat off of the plants. It's pretty, though. Daddy said you can't eat pretty."

Angel listened to her talk. To him, her voice was like music without instruments. He smiled and looked straight at her for the first time. He had never seen blonde hair up close before and he had never seen such pale skin.

"Angel help you walk," he said again. This time, it was a promise.

After a nice long visit, Rachel started to say goodbye, but Laura Dell decided that she and Angel could walk with them to their driveway. They walked along talking for another ten minutes. Angel pushed Neesie's chair while Neesie talked and talked. Every once in a while, she would ask Angel a quick question and he would say, "Yeah." And then, she would start talking again.

On the way home, Laura Dell noticed that Angel was very quiet, and he had a sad, serious look on his face. She said, "Angel, do you like Neesie?"

"Yeah."

"Well, is something wrong? You look so sad."

"Momma, Angel help Neesie."

Laura Dell said, "I'm sure you will, Sweetheart."

"Momma, Angel help Neesie walk again."

Angel put his arm around his mother and began to cry, his heart was broken for the little girl in the wheelchair.

Laura Dell didn't know what to do or what to say. Angel believed that he could help Neesie walk again, but Rachel had told her the doctors didn't think it was likely.

Her spine had been injured, and they couldn't repair it because of the location of the injury. It was too far down in her lower back. The technology didn't exist yet that could help Neesie to get well. And now, her little boy, who didn't understand some situations very well, wanted to help her walk again.

He might not understand everything in this human world, but he certainly understood the pain of compassion.

She kept her arm around her son's shoulder until they made it home. Angel hopped on his bicycle and began his ride around the yard. Around and around and around.

Chapter Sixteen

FOR THE REST OF THE summer, there was a set routine. At about three o'clock in the afternoon, Laura Dell would walk with Angel to Neesie's house so he could spend a couple of hours visiting with her. Laura Dell would stay sometimes and talk, but at other times, she would leave Angel there and drive into Cedar Ridge to pick up some groceries or pay bills. Angel was comfortable with staying with Neesie. He would usually push her out along the pathway around the fish pond and they would find a place in the shade. She would talk away, and Angel would sit and listen and give an occasional answer to one of her questions.

On rainy days, they would find a children's book and read to each other. Neesie could read much faster than Angel, but Angel knew the meanings and pronunciations of more words. The only time that their conversation was equal in time was when they were reading. Sometimes they would write, and sometimes they would color.

Rachel was impressed with Angel's penmanship. She also noticed that when he wrote a sentence, he was able to express his thoughts better than when he spoke. One afternoon, she pointed it out to Laura Dell. "Have you noticed that Angel writes in complete sentences?"

Of course, Laura Dell knew this. "Oh, yes. I have never accepted poor spelling or bad grammar from him when he writes. I hope that someday he will be able to speak in long sentences instead of short choppy ones, but who knows? His ability to learn is affected in different parts of his mind. I try not to get frustrated. I don't think he understands the concept of faking a disability. Some things he can pick up quickly. Others, he may never quite grasp. I try to notice how he acts when he is confronted with a new situation or idea."

Rachel said, "One thing I'm sure of, he understands friendship. He and Neesie get along so well. I think they will be a big help to each other in school."

Two weeks before school started, there was a meeting with the teacher. Since both Neesie and Angel were in the first grade and they had special needs, Laura Dell and Rachel met the teacher, Mrs. Henderson, together. They explained that the parents and their children were well acquainted and how Angel and Neesie hoped to help each other in class. Mrs. Henderson thought a moment and said, "You do understand that we can't allow Neesie to help Angel with his classwork, don't you?"

Rachel laughed, "Mrs. Henderson, I know Angel. In a few weeks, you might be using him as a teacher's aide. If he adjusts well socially, he will be the one you think of as a model student."

Mrs. Henderson said, "Oh, okay. If he is smart scholastically, then how is he autistic? What are his limited abilities?"

Laura Dell said, "He has difficulties with noise, but since it's going to be children making most of the noises, that might be a very small problem. If he becomes upset, you can put him in a quiet place and he will calm down quickly. Also, some things he learns differently. If he struggles with anything during class, you can send me a note about what it is and I'll work with him at home."

Mrs. Henderson said she could do that and they would see how it worked. Any adjustment shouldn't be a big problem.

She turned to Rachel and asked, "Now, is Neesie's wheelchair motorized?"

"No, it has to be pushed. But Angel can push it. As a matter of fact, he insists on pushing it. So, when you go to lunch or out to play or anywhere else, you won't have to worry about looking after Neesie. Unless it's up a steep slope or something like that, Angel will help Neesie. I don't think she will have much difficulty because of her wheelchair."

Mrs. Henderson said, "Do you know what? The wheelchair is good, because I was concerned about a heavy motorized wheelchair around the little first graders.

And how about her mental abilities? Is she going to need special attention, or does she learn on a normal scale?"

Rachel smiled, "She's fine, Mrs. Henderson. She hurt her back, not her head."

Mrs. Henderson reached across the table and squeezed Rachel's hand. "Please, Mrs. Daws, I know a few questions I am asking are hard and straight forward, but I want things to go smoothly for every one of my students. All of them are going to be different in their own ways. I will only have them for this one special year to teach, but I am going to love them all for the rest of my life."

Her voice was soft, but it was intense and sincere. She let go of Rachel's hand. Rachel whispered, "I'm sorry, Mrs. Henderson. I'm just very apprehensive about letting my little girl be out of my sight. To me, she's so fragile, and I couldn't stand it if..."

Mrs. Henderson handed Rachel a tissue. "She'll be fine, Mrs. Daws. Angel and I will make sure nothing happens to her."

That day, in that short meeting, a bond was formed between Rachel and Laura Dell and Mrs. Henderson. The two children were going to set out on their journey into life among people, and the three ladies were going to guide them and protect them closely.

When school did finally start, Mrs. Henderson seated Angel next to Neesie. The other students accepted the fact that Angel pushed her everywhere. Since most of them had never seen a wheelchair, whatever Angel and Neesie did was normal.

Neesie was her usual talkative self from the first day. She made friends immediately. Angel, who said only a few words each day, considered himself to be involved in all of Neesie's conversations and every new friend she made, he claimed as his own as well. Still, nobody pushed Neesie's chair but Angel.

Although his verbal skills were limited, Angel did well in the subjects that involved writing and he excelled in mathematics. At recess, he was uninterested in team sports. Although he was well coordinated, he didn't grasp the idea of competition. So when the class went out to the playground, he would push Neesie out and find a shady spot and sit patiently on the ground next to her and listen to her chat, giving the usual short response if she asked him anything. Sometimes, a few of the other students would come and sit around them and talk for the whole play period.

Mrs. Henderson never interrupted the little gatherings. She could see how both Neesie and Angel were gaining social skills. Learning those skills was just as important to all of her students as playing sports. Over the course of a lifetime, the free flow of conversation between six year old children probably meant more than sports and Mrs. Henderson instinctively knew it.

One day while Angel was at school, Laura Dell went into Mr. Green's store to grab a few items. Mr. Green said, "It sure is lonesome during the day without my little buddy coming by to shake my hand. Is he doing well at school?"

Laura Dell smiled a sad smile. "He's doing great. But, I'm lost in that big old house with nobody there but me. I'm going to have to find a hobby or something."

Mr. Green said, "Hey! Do you think you could help me in the store for a few hours a day? Like Angel said, I need to get this place straightened up. If you will work the counter, I can organize the stock."

"Well, if you really need somebody, I could work from the time Angel goes to school until about three o'clock. I can see if Rachel will let Angel stay with her for an hour or so. I mean, if you're serious."

Mr. Green said, "How about from ten until three, Monday through Friday? Anytime you need to be off, just ask. I can pay you ten dollars an hour, which isn't much, but you have to admit, it's a short drive to work."

Laura Dell said, "Let me talk it over with J. P. I think he'll go along with it. If anything happens at the school, I will be just across the road."

That night, Laura Dell told J. P. about the offer Mr. Green had made. J. P. said, "That's a couple of hundred a week. I don't know how long he can keep you there and make money, but he does need to straighten up his store. His place is a lawsuit waiting to happen."

Laura Dell said, "I can help him with some of the shelves when there are no customers in the store. Maybe he will gain a few customers when we have everything put in order."

J. P. said, "I think you should try it for a few weeks and see how it works. If Angel or Neesie need something, you can scoot across the street in no time."

The next Monday, Laura Dell became a store clerk. She and Mr. Green set a goal of November the fifteenth for having the store reasonably organized. That way, they would be more efficient when customers began their Thanksgiving shopping. If they could keep everything neat and accessible until New Year's Day, they might show a decent profit.

The work kept Laura Dell busy, but she wasn't very tired. Boredom had worn her out more than the store ever did.

Chapter Seventeen

THE NEXT FEW MONTHS FLASHED by without any major incidents. Thanksgiving week came and Laura Dell was able to work at the store while J. P. was off for the holiday. He and Angel made a Picnic area out under the big tree at the back corner of the field. They cooked weenies over an open fire. Angel agreed with his Papa that they were the best they had ever tasted. J. P. cleared the brush away from the creek bank and fixed Angel a fishing cane. After a while, they decided nothing was going to bite, so they spread a blanket in the grass and dozed in the afternoon sun of a late Autumn day.

Since the store was staying open late just before Thanksgiving, J. P. and Angel sat on the couch and watched a boxing match. Angel had never seen two men box. He said, "Papa, why those men dance without music?"

"They're not dancing son, they're boxing."

"What kind of dance is boxing?"

J. P. knew that Angel didn't see the effort the men were putting forth in the contest. He began a slow explanation. "Boxing is not dancing. They are trying to hit each other. They want to knock each other down."

Angel asked, "Both fall down at the same time?"

"No, one wants to knock the other one down without falling down himself."

"Which one knock down and which one fall down?"

J. P. smiled and looked at his son, "That's the fun part of watching. Nobody knows which one will get knocked down. The people cheer for the one they think will knock the other man down."

Angel watched another round. When it ended and a commercial came on, he said, "Me like to watch boxing dance. Angel not hit nobody."

J. P. said, "Son, they're not really mad at each other. It's a sport. It's a game. They get paid to box each other."

Angel said, "Oh."

The next round, one of the fighters knocked the other one down and out. The crowd cheered when the fight was over. As the winner strutted around the ring with his hands raised, Angel declared, "Angel learn boxing dance. Me box like him. Dance around and swing hands, pow! Pow! Pow!"

Angel jumped up from the couch and danced around like a boxer, punching the air and shifting his feet. He moved around the room, ducking and punching.

J. P. watched him, amazed at his quickness. "Dang, boy! You can dance like a boxer."

Angel danced all over the room, punching and ducking and shuffling his feet.

An idea formed in J. P.'s mind. Oh, Laura Dell was going to be mad about this, but J. P. was J. P., and sometimes he did stuff.

Laura Dell finally made it home at about eight o'clock. J. P. knew she needed her sleep, but as soon as they were in bed, he told her about Angel's boxing dance.

"You should have seen him, Laura Dell. He was all over the room! He has fast hands, and he's quick as a cat."

Laura Dell raised up on one elbow and growled at J. P. "If you think for one second that I'm going to let somebody hit my son, then you are out of your mind!"

"No, no, Laura Dell. I don't want him to box. I just want him to train like a boxer. He thinks it's a dance. We can fix up the extra room with a punching bag and a speed bag and a jump rope. And, no, I promise, he won't ever get into a ring with gloves on. It will just be for exercise during the winter."

"No!"

"Okay."

"You're going to do it, aren't you?"

"No."

"Then, what are you going to do?"

"Just one thing. Only one thing."

Laura Dell was gritting her teeth. "What one thing, J. P.?"

"Uhhh, well, I'm going to get the Rocky movie and let him watch it with me."

Laura Dell wrapped her pillow around her ears. "You drive me crazy, J. P. Everything is going good. Our whole world is nice and quiet and calm. But, no! I go to work one day and you watch a boxing match. The next thing I know, you want to turn one of the rooms into Madison Square Garden! No! I mean it, J. P.! No."

J. P. lay back on the bed with his hands behind his head and a dreamy smile on his face. "Okay," he said, lying like a dog.

Laura Dell rolled over on her side facing away from him. "A boxing angel, good Lord," she said as she blew out a long frustrated sigh.

The next day, J. P. was true to his statement of the night before. Angel sat by him on the couch while they ate pizza and watched Rocky. Just as J. P. expected, Angel was more interested in the training scenes than he was in the actual boxing match.

J. P. watched as Angel's full attention was focused on the footwork and the rhythm of the jump rope scenes. When he saw the speed bag, he let out a short wordless yell.

After the movie, J. P. asked him, "What did you think about that movie, Angel? Do you still want to be a boxer?"

"Angel not hurt nobody, but me hit that balloon. Pow, pow,pow,pow,pow! Me hit that big sack. Boom, boom, boom! Angel jump over that rope fast, too, Papa!"

J. P. smiled. "We don't have any of that stuff. Maybe you can tell Momma to get you some of it for Christmas. She probably doesn't know you want it."

"Okay, Papa, Angel tell Momma. Me not afraid of Momma like Papa."

J. P. said, "Now, boy."

Angel looked at his Papa with that sneaky look in his eyes and a little half smile on his face.

Chapter Eighteen

CHRISTMAS MORNING CAME AND ANGEL opened his gifts. There weren't many, and most of them were clothes. The family ate breakfast and started to get dressed for their visit to both of the grandparents' houses.

Angel couldn't find his shoes. He knew exactly where he had left them the night before and he was beginning to be upset about losing them.

J. P. said, "Why don't you look in the back room, son? They might be in there."

"Me not go in the back room. My shoes not there."

Laura Dell said, "I think I put them in there when I was moving stuff around. Go see if you can find them."

Angel said, "Okay." He walked towards the back as Laura Dell and J. P. followed along behind him, tiptoeing and hoping that he wouldn't look back and catch them.

When Angel opened the door to the room, there were the big punching bag, a speed bag, a jump rope, silk boxing shorts, little boxing gloves, and a robe! On a small table, there was a C D player. When J. P. pushed the play button, the theme from Rocky began to play. "Ho!", Angel shouted. He grabbed the shorts and pulled them over his pants, and then he put the robe on over his shirt. "Put the gloves on me, Papa!" Angel was already hopping around in time with the music.

J. P. slid the gloves over his hands, and even though they were very small gloves, they looked huge on Angel's hands.

Angel danced around throwing punches at the air. Laura Dell put her hand over her mouth and laughed. J. P. stood still, his eyes bright with pride. Angel walked over to the heavy bag and punched, "Humph, humph, humph." The gloves made quiet thuds as his little fists struck the canvas bag.

After punching the bag about twenty times, Angel was breathing heavily. He moved to the speed bag and gave it a pop. The bag bounced off of the top piece that held it and hit Angel in the forehead, knocking him backwards. J. P. laughed. Angel looked at his Papa and with a half grin said, "Punching bag hit back." Then he hit the speed bag again and the same thing happened. The third time, Angel leaned away from the bag as he punched. The bag missed his head.

Angel held his hands out for J. P. to pull the gloves off. He tried the jump rope, but it proved to be a difficulty. Angel would have to learn the timing of jumping rope with his feet and of punching the speed bag.

They let Angel play with his new toys for a few minutes before he had to finish getting ready for their Christmas day travels.

He did much better that year, being around the family members. The sound of so many voices didn't seem to upset him as much. He played with his cousins without hesitation, recognizing them as other children. They didn't make a big deal out of the fact that he didn't talk very often. His aunts and uncles spoke to him normally, not showing too much attention and not crowding in too close.

It was a good Christmas.

Within a couple of weeks, Angel taught himself to jump the rope. The speed bag was much harder for him to master, but after a couple of months, he was pounding out a quick beat as the theme from Rocky played along. He beat on the heavy bag as well, but his favorite activity was the shadow boxing and the footwork, and he always jumped the rope. At the end of every workout, he would always yell, "Adrianne! Adrianne!" That was his signal to let everyone know he had finished the session.

Laura Dell continued to work at the store after the new year began. Mr. Green found that he had room for more stock after he had everything put in its place. He added some canned goods to his grocery aisles and several new hardware items like pipe fittings and extension cords and a few hand tools. If the stock moved too slowly, at least it wouldn't ruin, and he could reorder whatever he sold quickly. When the extended neighborhood saw the new items, they made it a point to remember that it was at Mr. Green's store. They didn't have to drive to town to get the parts if they were needed urgently.

The long part of winter, which is from the middle of January until the middle of March seemed to drag by. If it wasn't cold, it was raining.

Neesie was spending six hours at school in her wheelchair without a break and by the time Rachel brought her home in the afternoon, she was in pain. Rachel would lay her on her back on a firm little bed and massage her legs. Then she would roll her over and rub her shoulders and back. Sometimes, this would cause Neesie to cry because the massages hurt pretty bad.

One day, Rachel was tired and when Neesie began to cry, she spoke sharply to her daughter. Angel, who usually stood by while Rachel rubbed Neesie's legs, stepped up next to Rachel and said, "Miss Rachel you want Angel to help? Me know how. Angel watch every day. Me can help."

"No, Sweetie, I'm just tired. It's been a long day for us all. The winter will be over soon and I hope the warm sun will help Neesie's bones."

"Me help and you can rest. Angel knows you're tired. Angel can tell."

Neesie said, "Mommy, let Angel try to rub my legs. If it hurts, I'll tell him to stop."

Rachel was tired and depressed. She had no energy and no patience left for her little girl. "Oh, alright," she said. "Here, Angel, you start at her ankles. Wrap your hands all the way around her leg like this."

Angel watched as Rachel showed him how to apply pressure, then move about an inch and apply pressure again. He understood her instructions and after a few minutes, he was massaging Neesie's legs as well as Rachel could have done it. This allowed Rachel time to sit down and rest before she started cooking their evening meal.

By the end of the week, Angel was able to give Neesie her afternoon massage. The only help he needed was when Neesie had to be rolled over. At the end of every massage, Angel would hold Neesie's hand and say in a quiet, assuring voice, "Angel help Neesie walk again. Angel help Neesie walk."

Some days, when Laura Dell would come to pick up Angel, he would be very quiet and somber. When she asked him if something was wrong, he would shake his head and say, "Angel help Neesie walk again."

There was no doubt in Laura Dell's mind that Angel was still dancing in his dreams, but now, she believed he had a partner. In his beautiful innocent little dreams, Angel was dancing with Neesie.

Chapter Nineteen

THE EXPECTED RETURN OF NEESIE'S father didn't happen. Military matters were not going well. Morale was low and Sergeant Daws was needed at his duty station, which was some place in a desert half way around the world.

When he called Rachel to tell her that it would be another year before he returned, she was devastated. He spoke to Neesie and it broke her heart as well.

The bright warm days of Spring couldn't cheer them up at all. A year of waiting and worrying over the absent husband and father didn't come to an expected end with a joyous reunion. There is a knowledge of danger that never leaves the mind of a person who is waiting for the return of a military loved one, and wars are hardly ever fought for freedom anymore. Bitter words are always waiting at the top of a person's throat, ready to be spoken if something goes wrong. To those who wait, the cause is not worth the potential loss. It's not worth the loneliness. It's never worth it. When a family member doesn't come home, or comes home maimed and scarred, they may never say a word in public, but during sleepless tear-filled nights, the brokenhearted survivors curse the masters of senseless war.

Laura Dell tried to find a way to cheer Rachel up. She knew that her friend was country raised, so the thought of planting a garden came to her mind. She bought a tiller.

The school year ended. Mr. Green didn't need her very often at the store, but when he did, Angel stayed with Neesie. One morning, Laura Dell called Rachel and asked her to come by. She needed some help with something. In a few minutes, Rachel came down the road, pushing Neesie in her wheelchair.

Laura Dell was standing outside looking at her new tiller. She waved Rachel over to her as Angel took Neesie's wheelchair and guided her to a shade tree.

"How do you start this thing? You said you were a farm girl. I don't know anything about it."

Rachel looked the tiller over. "Girl, you have bought yourself an expensive machine here." She checked the oil and the fuel, looked at the instructions that were printed on the engine cover, moved a couple of levers and gave the pull rope a quick jerk. It sputtered on the first pull and cranked on the second. Rachel let it run for a few seconds and then turned it off.

"Laura Dell, what are you going to do with this tiller?"

Laura Dell looked amused and happy. "If I can get you to help me, we're going to plant us a vegetable garden on the other side of that old apple tree."

Rachel looked at the tiller and looked out past the apple tree. "How big of a garden?"

"Big!"

"Half an acre?"

"Is that big?"

"Heck yeah, it's big. It will be all that we can handle."

Laura Dell said, "Well then, we are going to plant a half an acre."

Rachel said, "Let me see what kind of seeds you have."

They sat at the kitchen table and talked and planned the layout of the garden. Rachel explained to Laura Dell about buying small tomato plants already sprouted. She walked outside with her and showed her how to start and operate the tiller.

"I'll be back this evening before the sun goes down," Rachel said. "We can start turning the ground. When it gets too dark to plow, we'll call it a day."

Laura Dell said, "Great! I'll cook supper before you come over. We can all eat here after we get through."

The tiller was a digging machine. With Rachel's know how and Laura Dell's enthusiasm, their garden was plowed and planted within a week. Both of the ladies felt their skins turn brown and their muscles harden. J. P. helped in the afternoons as he was needed, but Laura Dell made sure he understood the project belonged to Rachel and her. He was fine with that.

The garden grew, and Rachel's spirits seemed to lift along with it. Both families picked from the garden as they needed the vegetables, but it soon became obvious that there was way too much being produced.

One day, during the ladies' usual visit to the store, their conversation with Mr. Green turned to produce.

"I don't know where I am going to find fresh vegetables," Mr. Green said. "All of my stock comes from greenhouses, and they are about to play out. They come in early in the year, but greenhouse vegetables lose their quality about the time folks start craving okra and corn and stuff." He looked at his produce shelves, "And to tell you the truth, greenhouse vegetables don't have near the taste that garden raised do."

Rachel looked at Laura Dell and then, at the same time, they said, "We have a garden!"

Mr. Green said, "Can I get some stock to put in my store?"

Rachel said, "We'll pick it in the morning and bring it down here. You see if it sells, and if it does, give us half."

The deal was struck. Rachel had a purpose again. Laura Dell was glad to see her friend smiling and involved. It was clear to her that Rachel was a farmer.

They expanded the size of the garden and planted a second set of tomatoes, as well as beans and okra. The rest of the summer, Rachel worked the garden, tilling and picking and pulling weeds. Sometimes she would come down and hand Neesie off to Angel and spend a couple of hours by herself in the garden. Laura Dell understood that Rachel didn't always need her there. Sometimes, quiet helped much more than conversation ever could.

And so another Summer passed. The children grew. Angel still talked in short choppy sentences. Neesie still didn't show any signs of gaining use of her legs again. When her back was hurting, Angel would come to her house and massage her legs and arms and shoulders and back. Always, before he helped her back into the wheelchair, he would hold her hand and softly say, "Angel help Neesie walk again."

Every other voice in her life had almost stopped saying anything about walking. In her heart, she held on to the promise of a stuttering little Angel. She was going to walk.

Chapter Twenty

THE CALENDAR TURNED. LAURA DELL helped Mr. Green through the holiday season. One day, while Laura Dell was working at the store and J. P. was in the kitchen making a quick lunch, Angel started yelling. J. P. ran into the living room to see what had happened.

There was a circus on the television and Angel was watching a clown juggle. "Papa! What is that? Is that dance, Papa? Look, Papa! That man crazy!"

"He's not crazy, son. He's a clown."

The clown was juggling balls. It looked like he had six going at one time. His hands were a blur, and he was pretending to stumble and almost drop them as he moved around the stage. Angel watched with his mouth open. When the clown would pretend to lose his balance, Angel would yell. Everything was real to him.

"He's not going to drop them, son. It's part of the act."

"What act?"

J. P. said, "The dance that he's doing. It's part of his dance."

Angel never looked away from the television. "Why he paint his face? Why he wear funny pants?"

J. P. said, "It's part of the act. It's his costume."

"What does costume mean?"

"Special clothes he wears while he does the juggling dance." J. P. thought of something similar to use as a comparison. "Like your shorts and your robe when you do your boxing dance."

Angel said, "Oh." The juggling portion of the show ended. Angel turned to J. P. and said, "Papa, Angel learn juggling dance."

J. P. was doubtful. "I don't know about that. Juggling is hard to learn. It takes a special talent to be able to..."

"Me learn juggling dance!"

"But, Angel, not everybody can juggle."

"Me learn. Angel get balls and juggle dance. Angel do Casper dance. Angel do boxing dance. Angel do juggling dance."

J. P. sensed that Angel was getting upset. "Angel, you have to have a special kind of ball to juggle. They have to be a certain size, and they have to be soft so you won't break anything while you're learning how to juggle."

"Papa go get me juggle dance balls. Angel learn now!"

"I can't go get them now. I don't even know who to buy them from."

Angel's face turned red. He pointed his finger towards the door. "Angel go see Mr. Green. He sell me juggle dance balls."

J. P. tried not to laugh. "Young man, you're not going to see Mr. Green or anybody else. The world doesn't stop just because you saw a clown juggling on the t. v."

"Angel ride bicycle to store." He started for the door, but J. P. scooped him up in his arms. Angel started kicking and swinging his fists.

J. P. sat down on the couch and held Angel tightly on his lap. Angel was strong and J. P. was struck several times by a foot or a fist. It was all he could do to keep his temper, but he never said a cross word to Angel. After about five minutes of pulling and kicking, Angel finally stopped struggling. He was still mad, though. As soon as he had recovered enough to speak, he said, "Papa, you mean! Angel tell Momma when she gets home. Momma get mad at Papa for being mean. Momma holler at Papa! Momma go buy me some juggle dance balls."

"You're not going to tell on me. I'm your best bud. You wouldn't get me in trouble with Momma."

Angel looked up over his shoulder at his Papa, "Uhuh, Angel tell Momma. Momma holler at Papa because Papa mean." He tried to wiggle loose, but the effort was wasted. J. P. had a firm grip.

J. P. said, "Now, boy, I am going to make us some lunch. After you eat, you have to take your nap."

"Angel going to store. Me tell Momma and Mr. Green. Papa mean."

"I am going to get up and you are going to sit right here. Christmas is almost here. If you try to leave, I promise you, you won't get anything. I was going to tell Momma to get you a new bicycle for Christmas, but since we aren't buds anymore, I might tell her to get you some tee shirts with real tight necks that you can't get your head through, and when you get stuck in one, I am not going to help you get loose!"

Angel gasped. "No, Papa!"

"Well, you are going to tell Momma that I'm mean, anyway. I may as well put your head in a tee shirt."

"No! You not put Angel's head in a shirt."

"Are you going to sit right there until I fix our lunch?"

Angel folded his arms across his chest and pouted.

J. P. went into the kitchen and warmed up a couple of bowls of soup, keeping a close eye on Angel. When he called Angel into the kitchen to eat, Angel didn't say a word. But it seemed like he cheered up a little bit with every bite. By the time he finished eating, Angel was his usual self.

He said, "Angel not tell Momma you mean."

J. P. started to tease him a little, but he decided that was a bad idea. He said, "Good, because I don't want to tell her that you can't have a new bicycle for Christmas."

Angel said, "Good. Angel go take nap."

That night when J. P. and Laura Dell were in bed, she snuggled up to him and whispered, "Will you tell me a secret, J. P.?"

"Of course I will, Baby. What kind of a secret do you want to know?"

She put her hand on his cheek and softly said, "It's the kind of a secret only a real man like you would know."

J. P. cleared his throat. Now he was getting nervous. In his mind, he was going back through the last couple of weeks and trying to remember a conversation in which he had bragged more than he should have. He had said a few outlandish things that he could recall, but nothing he couldn't talk his way out of. Deciding to play innocent, he said, "What kind of secret do you want to know about?"

Laura Dell put her lips right up next to his ear and whispered, "What....are....juggle dance balls?"

J. P. sat up in the bed. "Oh, that's funny, Laura Dell! I didn't know what you were going to ask me."

Laura Dell was laughing so hard she couldn't catch her breath. "Well," she said between fits of laughter, "well, what are they?" And she collapsed against the bed again. "Aaahahhahahaaa! Aaaahahahaaa!"

J. P.'s face was red. He looked at the far wall and said, "I'm not going to tell you."

Laura Dell whispered, "But Baby, I really want to know. You can tell me. I'll understand."

J. P. started laughing with her. That son of theirs never stopped thinking. If he thought it was a dance, then he was going to learn how to do it.

He explained to Laura Dell about the juggler on television. He told her about the big argument. Laura Dell listened with a smile.

"You are a mean Papa," she said. "All he wanted was some juggle dance balls."

J. P. said, "I've been thinking about what size of a ball we should get. A handball should be about right. His hands are too small for a tennis ball."

Laura Dell asked, "Do you think he can learn to juggle?"

"Nope, but if we get him a couple of packs of handballs for Christmas, he can try. Of course, he'll need a clown outfit to go with the handballs."

"A clown outfit?" Laura Dell acted surprised, but she wasn't.

J. P. said, "Yep, a clown outfit, complete with a frizzly multicolored wig. It's part of the juggle ball dance. He has to have a clown outfit."

Laura Dell said, "I'll see what I can find. I am guessing there should be a theme song to play as well."

J. P. said, "Tears of a Clown by Smoky Robinson. Oh, and only v-neck tee shirts from now on."

Laura Dell fell asleep wondering if she should hide a voice recorder in the house while she was working at the store. That way some of Angel's questions would make more sense.

The days after Christmas were filled with the sound of music from the back room. First, it was the smooth voice of Smoky along with his jingling music. They could hear the frustrated exclamations from Angel as he tried to learn to juggle. When they heard the brassy introduction music to Rocky, they knew their son had decided to take his frustration out on his punching bags.

After calling, "Adriannne! Adriannne!", Angel would emerge from his private little world looking hot and thirsty.

All through the long months of Winter, Angel tried to learn to juggle. He never said if he was getting the hang of it, and his parents never asked.

Chapter Twenty One

SPRINGTIME CAME AS IT ALWAYS does. Angel had grown in a sudden spurt. His ability to accomplish schoolwork was equal to his classmates, but his language skill, when speaking, remained unchanged. This caused Laura Dell some concern. She wondered if the speech disability would have a negative effect on his adult life. She expressed her concerns to Dr. Padgett.

"He is passing all of his classes, even writing and English grammar. I don't understand why he's still talking baby talk."

Dr. Padgett asked, "Are you sure it's baby talk?"

Laura Dell thought for a minute. "His conversations are always short. He never talks about anything complicated. He thinks in straight lines, I guess. What he can see or what he has just seen are all that matters to him."

Dr. Padgett said, "Oh, he's probably doing a lot more thinking than he is talking. What does he say when you tell him you love him?"

"Usually nothing. Sometimes he nods or says okay. I'm not sure he understands what love means."

Dr. Padgett had years of experience with autistic children. She believed there was one thing common to all of them. They knew whether or not they were loved. Relationships hold a deep meaning for them. Every person, every voice is identified according to how they interact with the autistic child. Emotions are usually simple and solid. This is my friend. This is my provider. This is my protector. This is my teacher. This is my comforter. This is my confidant. People hold multiple titles according to what is going on at the moment, but the child sees those around him according to simple identities.

Dr. Padgett said, "Laura, he may be struggling with self expression and that could be a disability he can't overcome, but we need to see if he can increase his spoken vocabulary."

"I don't know how. He only talks if he is excited about something or if you ask him a question. And then he gives a short answer. He's happy if he only says a dozen words in a day. He is not compelled from the inside to talk."

Dr. Padgett thought he probably was. She believed he wanted to communicate, but something was blocking him. "How about this? One day, when nothing is going on and there's nobody around, I want you to start asking him questions, one right after another. Start digging. See if you can pull something out that he's struggling with."

"What kind of questions?"

Dr. Padgett searched through her memories. It was an important question and she wanted to give Laura Dell a useful answer. "The next time something catches his attention, something new, ask him what he thinks it is. Make it something important, not a toy, but an idea or human behavior, something like that. Take your time and watch for a chance. You'll know the time when it shows up."

Laura Dell thanked Dr. Padgett and promised to call as soon as the chance came. After they said their good-byes, Dr. Padgett sat for several minutes before focusing her attention on anyone else. She made some notes in Angel's file before putting it away.

On almost all levels, Angel was high functioning, but the inability to communicate well canceled most of his physical abilities out. She knew that one of the hard challenges for autistic people is that sometimes they come to a dead end. Some parts of their minds and bodies just don't function. This appeared to be so with Angel.

There are times when changes come all at once, and good changes enhance everybody's lives. That Summer was a time of good changes.

The war ended. Rachel's husband came home. When Laura Dell and J. P. and Angel went to visit the complete Daws family, he greeted them warmly.

"Come in, come in. I feel like I already know y'all. I am Benji, but everybody calls me Sarge or Boots. You are J. P., right? And Laura Dell? And you have to be Angel."

They all shook hands including Angel. He looked into Boot's eyes and said, "You home now. Neesie happy."

Boots tried to smile, but tears immediately began to flow down his cheeks. He called Rachel over to chat while he left the room. After a few minutes, he returned.

There was the usual first meeting conversation. Boots had been given three months leave. His enlistment was coming to an end. The decision about whether or not to reenlist was a hard one. He could probably stay stateside for six years and retire with a good pension. He was a master sergeant. The pay was good, but over two years in a combat zone had taken its toll. Like all soldiers, he wanted peace.

They sat out by the fish pond and talked a lot about nothing. Rachel wanted to buy a small tractor and plant a much larger garden. Boots knew how to operate one and she wanted to learn as well.

J. P. invited Boots over the next day to look at the field and decide if he wanted to fool with a big garden or not. Boots was tall and lean and physically fit, but J. P. could see something in his eyes, something he almost understood.

The next Saturday, Rachel and Boots came walking into the driveway. Angel and Neesie found a place under their favorite shade tree. Laura Dell and Rachel went into the house, and J. P. asked Boots if he wanted to take a look at the garden.

Boots looked around, almost without interest and said, "Sure, we can do that I guess."

When they passed the old apple tree, J. P. noticed that Boots was looking more at the creek than he was at the garden.

J. P. said, "Let's just keep walking. I'll show you the garden later. I want to give you something."

Boots said, "Okay, but you don't have to give me anything. I owe you and your family more than I can ever repay."

They walked along the old farm road, not saying anything. Boots stayed close to the smooth flowing creek. He stopped several times to watch a fish swim along close to the bank. He gazed at the ridge as they approached the corner of the property. Finally, when they came to the little picnic area at the base of the mountain where rapid little streams came from several directions and joined together to form Easy Creek, J. P. said, "Have a seat, Boots."

Boots took the chair closest to the creek bank. He sat and watched the ever flowing current. Birds sang in the brush and in the high limbs of the beech trees. There was a light breeze. Other than those few sounds, everything was quiet.

J. P. said, "Boots, this is yours. This is your place. You don't have to ask or call or anything. You come here day or night. Camp out, get drunk, holler, cuss, pray, laugh, cry, whatever you want to do. If you want to talk, I'm here. If you want to be left alone, nobody is going to bother you. Fish, wade, run the ridges, it's yours. It's your sanctuary."

Boots looked at J. P., his eyes full of gratitude. "It's beautiful. Rachel has described it to me, but I couldn't see it. I couldn't hear it or smell it or feel it."

J. P. said, "I've never been away from home, never been away from my family more than a week. I don't know how you feel, but I know it's going to take a while to change from a man in a war to a man in a field full of watermelons."

Boots laughed a quick laugh. "Well, I'm glad to have a chance to stand in a watermelon patch again. There's not much free soil left in the world."

He was quiet for a long time. J. P. wondered if he should leave and let him sit alone. Finally, Boots asked, "You got red eyed bass in this creek?"

"There's a few."

Boots said, "When there was a sandstorm, and when it was so cold we couldn't go out, that's what I did. In my mind, I waded little creeks and caught red eyes. I remember every little bend in the creek where I used to fish, how the branches hung over to make a shade, where the water cut under overhanging rocks, the logs across the current where the whirlpools formed. I dreamed I could feel that cold fresh water up to my calves. Man, I could see the little wake along the top of the pool when that joker came out to grab my lure." He stopped talking for a few seconds, a sad smile on his face. "You can't feel the pull when you set the hook, though. I would always jump and wake up when I set the hook."

J. P. said, "You can feel it now, Boots."

Boots drew in a deep, content breath of fresh air. He stood up, looked at the creek one more time and said, "Let's go look at that garden."

Chapter Twenty Two

BOOTS BOUGHT THE TRACTOR. THE one acre garden became a four acre garden. Boots knew what he was doing. The vegetables grew fast and thick. Midsummer brought bushels. Mr. Green and Boots sold at his store while Rachel sold from a truck in town in Cedar Ridge.

Few people noticed that there was a part of Boots that was still at war, but J. P. did. Late one afternoon, when Boots was standing out at the picnic area by the creek, J. P. walked out to sit with him. When he came up, he noticed that Boots was staring into the stream. His hands were trembling, only slightly, but J. P. noticed. He spoke well before he came too close, "Hey, Boots."

Boots turned around and flashed a nervous smile. "J. P., I was just thinking. I have to make a decision in a couple of weeks. The army is going to want to know which way I am going." He looked around like he was trying to get his bearings.

J. P. said, "Well, one thing's in your favor. The war's over."

Boots said, "Yeah, and we lost. We lost our boys, and we lost our equipment, and we spent a whole lot of our country's money for no reason."

J. P. said, "Maybe the world is a safer place because of what y'all did." The statement was so empty that it fell out of the air and didn't even bounce.

Boots sat down in a chair and put both hands on his forehead. He said, "I can probably get a duty station close enough to drive. Or I guess they would let me recruit until my retirement comes up. I don't want to coast in, though."

He looked around again, as though he was lost, or maybe he was searching for something he couldn't quite see yet.

J. P. didn't know if he should say anything. Boots was fighting a battle on the inside. Finally, J. P. asked, "Have you prayed about it?"

Boots said, "Yeah, but it doesn't feel like there's any-body listening. It feels like I'm small, like I'm not import-ant to God right now."

Boots stood up again and walked back to the creek, looking into the current. "What do I do, J. P.? What am I supposed to do now? I can put that uniform back on for a few more years, but nobody knows if there will be another war during that time. I can tell the army I'm done, but who's going to train our boys how to fight and stay alive if our veterans all retire?"

J. P. said, "Boots, that's a hard decision. Why don't we bring it before the whole church Sunday morning and ask everybody to pray about it? You need help and I believe God will help you."

Even though Boots wasn't the kind of man you hugged, J. P. put his arm over his shoulder and said, "You're not by yourself, Buddy. Don't ever think you're by yourself."

Boots nodded. "Let's go home. Maybe Rachel's got supper cooked."

They walked along the farm road back to the yard, not talking and not hurrying. Boots said, "See you tomorrow," and went up the road towards his house. J. P. watched him until he faded into the dusk. He knew that Boots was stuck at a crossroads in his mind. He felt a lump in his own throat. How long does the noise of war echo in the heart of a soldier? Maybe forever, he didn't know.

The next Sunday, Boots was at church. When the service ended and the pastor asked if all hearts were clear, Boots stood up from his seat and approached the altar. He said, "Preacher, as you know, I have spent over two years fighting a war. My leave is about to end and I need to decide whether to keep being a soldier or not. My family needs me as much as my country does. I want the church to pray for me that I will make the right decision, because I'm not sure what I should do."

The pastor reached into a drawer in the podium and pulled out a bottle of olive oil. He stepped down to where Boots was standing and said, "Church, I want you to reach your hands this way. This brother is one of our warriors and he has suffered wounds that we can't see, amen? Now, he has to decide if his time as a guardian of our nation is over or if there's one more mission for him to accomplish.

Brother Boots, you want to go where God sends you, don't you?" Boots nodded. "And you want to stay where God tells you to stay, don't you?" Boots nodded again.

The preacher took the top off of the bottle of olive oil. He pulled a handkerchief out of his pocket and poured some of the oil on it. He said, "Church, and I mean everyone that's here, I want you to reach your hands this way and pray with me for this man. Lord, God of all creation, we bring before you this good man, a father, a husband, a friend, and a soldier." The preacher placed the anointed cloth on top of Boots' head. "Let your will be done in this man's life! Let his decisions be right! Let his path become clear! Let his heart and mind be strong! Cast out doubt! Cast out confusion! Guide him, God! Guide him, now!"

Boots raised both of his hands above his head. "Show me the way, Lord," he called. "Show me the way."

Rachel ran from her seat and grabbed her husband. Neesie sat in her wheelchair with Angel holding her hand. She was weeping, sobbing.

A great shout of prayer and praise suddenly rose from the congregation. The spirit of God moved. The power of God moved.

This was a quiet church, but on this Sunday morning, for the sake of one good man's soul, the Comforter answered a call. The time of prayer lasted at least five minutes and when the church was quiet again, the preacher returned to the pulpit and said, "Well! I believe God heard your prayer for guidance, Brother Boots! I believe God heard a whole lot of prayers in these last few minutes. Before we dismiss, I want to say this, there are times when it seems like there's nobody in the spirit world listening when you pray, but God is always there. You don't have to feel him. He's not going to give you a sign just because you ask for one, but He's there, and He hears you. Now, church, I want you to go in the spirit of God and be joyful. Amen."

That afternoon, Angel came and sat down next to his mother. "Momma, what was that stuff the preacher poured on a rag and wiped on Boots?"

Here was the moment she was waiting for and Laura Dell recognized it immediately.

"That was olive oil, son. When preachers say a special prayer, they anoint a cloth and put it on the person they are praying for."

"What's anoint mean?"

"That means to pour it on something for healing. You know, like in the psalm, He anoints my head with oil."

Angel said, "Oh."

Laura Dell put her arm around Angel. "What did you think when the whole church started praying at once?"

"Angel thought it was beautiful! Me wanted to dance. Praying sounded like singing."

"Did you want to pray, too?"

Angel looked up into his mother's eyes. "Me did pray, Momma."

Laura Dell said, "I didn't hear you praying."

"Angel don't pray out loud much."

"Why don't you pray out loud? God wants to hear you pray just like everybody else."

Angel held his mother's hand and squeezed it. He motioned for her to lean over so he could whisper in her ear. She leaned down and listened.

Very, very quietly, Angel said, "Angel can't say."

Laura Dell whispered back, "Why can't you say?"

Still whispering, he said, "Me not know. Angel can hear and understand. Angel can feel when somebody happy or sad. Angel can love. Angel can get mad sometimes. Angel can write. But, Momma, Angel can't say. Words not come out for Angel. Not no time, never. Words not never come out for Angel. See, Momma? Angel can't say."

She understood. She wrapped him in her arms for a long time. "It's okay," she said. "Maybe someday we will figure out a way to help you talk."

For a long time, Angel didn't say anything. When he did, he changed the subject. "Momma, you buy Angel some olive oil?"

Surprised, Laura Dell asked, "Why do you want some olive oil?"

Angel shrugged his shoulders. He hopped up and ran out through the door.

Laura Dell looked out and saw him exactly where she thought he would be. He was riding his bicycle around and around and around.

Chapter Twenty Three

BOOTS MADE HIS DECISION. THERE was an opening at the nearest army base for an NCO instructor. His time in combat made him the most qualified candidate for the job. The army guaranteed his time of service there would last until he retired. It was an hour and a half drive, so he was given a room on the base. He could drive home on Friday afternoon and come back to the base on Monday morning. If he had an afternoon off, he could come home during the week. On the first day of October, he was back in uniform. The farm work had kept him in shape and within a week he was barking orders, teaching, remembering what usually works and what doesn't during combat. He felt like he was where God wanted him to be. He was happy. The nation needed front line soldiers that knew how to lead and keep their men alive and healthy. His work was a high calling.

For Angel and Neesie, the school year rolled along. Neesie did well, but Angel's grades began to fall slightly. In mathematics, he was excellent, and he did alright in science. Anything having to do with the English language was a problem. History, literature, and grammar were overwhelming his mind.

Laura Dell visited his teachers. They didn't have any answers. They didn't even have any suggestions. Angel would receive the grades he earned until he finished the fifth grade. What he learned at Easy Creek Elementary School in the next two years would be the knowledge he carried into middle school at Cedar Ridge.

Laura Dell worked with Angel on his most difficult subjects for half an hour on Tuesdays and Thursdays before bedtime. Since the tests were usually on Friday, it helped some. He was passing, but barely.

Neesie's back pain came back as soon as school started. Angel took over her massages completely, having grown strong enough to help her out of her wheelchair and onto the massage bed. Somehow, instinctively, he developed a unique method of rubbing her limbs and her shoulders and spine.

"Me start from middle," he said, "then work from middle out to sides. Angel not rub too hard. Angel make everything work right again. Me help Neesie walk again."

To Neesie, there was no other masseuse in the world. Angel's massage method helped her relax. The knotted muscles in her body fell into their correct positions as the pain disappeared.

Angel rode his bicycle to Neesie's on the weekends. She could roll herself around in her wheelchair now because Angel's massages help her muscles to develop, and she was growing in size as well, but sometimes Angel pushed her just because he still wanted to.

One Saturday morning, Angel had a bag hanging over his handlebars when he rode to Neesie's house. He hopped off of his bicycle and ran into the kitchen where Neesie and her family were eating breakfast.

Boots was sitting at the table when Angel came flying in. He looked over his shoulder and said, "Boy, you need to knock before you come into somebody's house."

Angel said, "No, Boots. Angel not knock. This is something important! Me show Neesie something new. Me show all!"

Rachel laughed and said, "What is it, Angel? Show it to us."

Angel said, "Okay, but you not talk while I show, because it's a dance. New Angel dance."

He opened his bag and pulled out a tape player and plugged it into the wall. He set the tape player in a chair. Then, he pulled out some baggy bright green striped pants and put them on. As he was putting his multi-colored wig on his head, Boots leaned over and whispered to Rachel, "What's he doing?"

Rachel whispered back, "I think he's going to dance," and giggled.

Angel looked at her and said, "Please, audience no talk!"

Neesie sat in her wheelchair, smiling, but not saying a word.

Angel pulled six small balls out of his bag. He handed three of them to Boots and said, "When Angel give signal, you toss one ball. Every time Angel do like this, you toss one ball." He gave a quick nod. "That my signal. You toss ball."

Boots said, "Okay."

Angel mashed the play button on his tape player and the jingling intro to Tears of a Clown began to play quite loudly. Angel said, "Heeeere goes!" And, he tossed one ball into the air and caught it with the same hand. He pointed at Neesie and smiled, frozen in a silly clown like pose. Then, he tossed the ball up again, and the next two were suddenly in the air, whirling in a quick, tight circle.

Angel danced around, his feet going in all directions. The three balls circled his head. They flew behind him as he spun around and caught them without breaking rhythm with the music. His feet moved with the pace of the song. Suddenly, he stopped. Nothing about him moved except his hands. The balls began to climb in a large fat circle, almost hitting the ceiling. He gave Boots a quick glance, "Get readyyyy, Boots!"

A quick nod and Boots tossed a ball to Angel. It blended in with the pattern of the other three. Another nod and the fifth ball popped into the circle. Angel nodded again. When Boots tossed the last ball, Angel seemed to dodge to the side. It looked like he missed, but somehow, that ball came out from behind his shoulder and found its place in the circle. Angel stood perfectly still, juggling all six balls as the music of the song faded out. When the song ended, he said, "Heads up!"

He tossed one ball to Boots, one to Rachel, and one to Neesie. He caught the other three in his hands and tossed one into the air, spun around and caught it and froze, absolutely still. "Angel do juggle dance," he said, and smiled.

His audience sat unmoving in their chairs, their mouths hanging half open. Finally, Rachel said, "I have never in my life seen anything like that."

Boots said, "Now, what's it called?"

Angel was taking off his wig and his pants. He folded the pants and put them in the bag along with the wig. "Juggle dance," he said. "Give Angel balls back, please."

Everybody handed him a ball. He said, "Neesie, you like juggle dance?"

Neesie clapped her hands together and said, "It's beautiful and it's funny and it goes so fast! My eyes couldn't keep up with your hands. Oh, it was good. It was good!"

Angel said, "You finished breakfast?"

Neesie nodded. "Let's go out to the fish pond and feed the fish."

Angel pushed her wheelchair away as she started talking about everything at once. Rachel heard Angel say, "Yeah," as they went out the back door.

Boots watched them as they went out. He said, "There's something unusual about that child. He's different."

Rachel smiled as she cleared the table. She took Angel's bag and set it on the table. "Yeah, he's autistic."

Boots said, "He's more than that. He's an angel of some kind. He's an angel."

Chapter Twenty Four

ON CHRISTMAS DAY THAT YEAR, J. P. gave Angel a special gift. It was a puppy. He explained to Angel that he was the one who would take care of the puppy, to feed and water it and to take it for a walk several times a day.

Angel watched it for a few minutes and said, "Papa, Angel don't want a puppy."

The puppy was rolling around on the floor playing with a soft toy. J. P. said, "Yes, you do. You just don't know it yet. That puppy's going to be your best friend in a few months."

Angel looked at his Papa. "Neesie is my best friend. Everybody knows." He smiled and said, "Papa, you silly sometimes."

J. P. said, "Well, if you don't take care of this puppy and train it, then I'm going to give it to Neesie and it will be her best friend. So, you better take care of it."

"Okay, Papa. Angel teach puppy."

J. P. said, "Now son, this breed of dog is called a Blue Heeler, and they love to learn tricks. They want to work together with people all of the time. You have to start training her right away. The first thing we have to do is give her a name. What does she look like to you, Angel?"

Angel looked at the puppy, but didn't pick her up. She was dark along her back and shoulders, fading to dark ticks set in white hair along her legs. "She looks like night coming down," he said. "Like almost dark time, but not yet."

Laura Dell said, "How about Nightshade? Is that what she looks like, the first shade of darkness after the sun goes down?"

Angel said, "Yeah."

And so the puppy was named Nightshade, but they all called her Shady from the very first day. She had a little kennel to sleep in, and she was quiet for the first couple of nights. But, after she became attached to Angel, she cried so loud that Angel put her on the foot of his bed and covered her up with a small blanket.

She followed him all around the rooms, pulling at the bottoms of his pants legs. When Angel went to school, she lay in her kennel watching the kitchen door. She danced around his feet while he punched on the punching bags. She ran around and around while he was jumping rope. She chased his juggling balls if he dropped one and sat still, watching for the next one to fall.

Spring came, and Angel pushed Neesie out to the picnic area one sunny afternoon. Shady followed along, hopping around in the grass, sometimes running ahead and almost falling into the creek a couple of times.

Angel parked Neesie's chair where she could see the water flowing along.

Neesie said, "Angel, this flowing water reminds me of how quickly time goes by. Next year, we'll be going to middle school. There's going to be a whole lot more kids there. We will make new friends, too. I hope I make some nice friends, don't you?"

Angel said, "Yeah."

Neesie continued with her usual chatter. "Time went by so fast, I forgot to start walking again, so I guess I'll still be in this dumb old wheelchair when we start school. You'll still push me, won't you, Angel? I mean, I can push myself, but I like having you there with me. You've always been there, right behind me, so I don't know how it's going to feel when you're not there anymore. You will stay with me, at least for the first year, won't you, Angel?"

Angel said, "Yeah."

Neesie watched the water as it rolled by. After a long silence, she looked up into Angel's eyes. She grabbed his arm, just above his elbow and said, "Angel, I can't remember what it felt like to walk. I can remember running and laughing, but I don't know how I moved my legs and feet anymore."

Angel said, "Before long, Angel help Neesie walk."

"You will?"

Angel said, "Yeah."

Neesie held on to his arm for a while. Finally, she said, "Then, I am going to help you do something."

"What you help Angel do?"

I am going to teach you to say "I."

Angel jerked his arm away from Neesie's hand. "Me not say I. Me say me and me say Angel, but not I."

"I think I understand why you never say I, and I am going to help you say it."

Angel raised his voice a little to Neesie, which he had never done before, "Angel not say I!"

Neesie reached and grabbed his other hand and held it. "Angel, I am your friend. I know you better than anyone in the whole world, and I know why you can't say I."

Angel almost jerked his hand away again, but he couldn't make himself. He said, "Why Angel not say I?"

"Because you can't figure out when you are supposed to say I and when you are supposed to say me."

Angel said, "Tell me when Angel say I and when Angel say me."

Neesie said, "Okay, listen real close and if you have to think for a minute before you talk, that's not a problem. And if you get it wrong every once in a while, don't get discouraged. We can practice without anyone else knowing. Are you ready?"

Angel said, "Yeah."

"When you are doing something for somebody, then you say, 'I'. When somebody is doing something for you, then you say 'me'. Like if you are pushing my chair you will say, 'I am pushing Neesie's chair'. If one day I can walk and I am pushing you in my chair, you will say, 'Neesie is pushing me', got it?"

Angel mumbled, "Yeah."

Neesie said, "Good. I want to go home, now. I wonder who will push my chair."

Angel said, "Angel push...."

Neesie cut him off. "Nope, you know what to say. Say, 'I will.'"

Angel felt his face turn hot all the way up to his forehead. "I will push Neesie's chair."

Neesie shouted, "Yea! You did it!"

Angel said, "Yeah."

Shady hopped and ran all the way back to the house with them. Neesie talked and talked. She couldn't see Angel's blushing face.

"I am pushing Neesie's chair," he thought as he walked along, barely hearing her words and barely feeling his feet touching the ground.

Chapter Twenty Five

IT WAS DURING THE SUMMER of that year, when Angel was twelve years old and Neesie was eleven, that Angel felt a small bump under the skin on Neesie's lower back. He ran his thumb over the place, and Neesie said, "Ouch! What was that? Did you stick me with something?"

Angel said, "No, Angel found a bump."

Neesie corrected him, "I found a bump."

"I found a bump on your backbone. Maybe Angel tell, uh, maybe I tell Rachel."

Neesie said, "No, Angel. If you tell her, she'll take me to the doctor and they will put me in the hospital. Let's put some medicine on it and see if it will go away. I don't want to go to the hospital. I have heard Mommy talking to the doctors. They don't believe I will walk again, but I do. You believe, too, don't you, Angel?"

Angel said, "Yeah." He finished the massage without touching the bump on her spine again.

Although she didn't need a massage every day in the Summer because she could get into and out of her chair during the day, Angel came to give her one the next afternoon. When he began to rub her back, he pulled a small bottle of olive oil out of his pocket. He showed it to Neesie and said, "This is olive oil. Angel anoint the place on your back like Preacher at church. Angel ask God to help Neesie walk."

Neesie said, "Are you sure? I mean, talking to God and anointing somebody who is sick, isn't that just for preachers?"

"Angel knows how. Angel, uh, I watch preacher every time. We ask God to make Neesie well. We ask God to help Neesie walk. Maybe somebody else not believe Neesie walk, but Neesie believes and Angel believes, so we ask God in Jesus. Amen."

Neesie said, "Amen."

Angel poured some olive oil onto the palm of his hand and rubbed his hands together. Then, very gently, he massaged the place on Neesie's spine where the bump was located.

Neesie wasn't surprised when she felt the pain that shot up and down her back. She didn't complain even though it really hurt. The pain went away quickly as Angel rubbed her back and shoulders.

That night, she slept better than she ever had, not waking up because of any discomfort. When she saw Angel the next day, she said, "I think that olive oil helped. Bring it every time you give me a massage."

Angel said, "Okay."

After a few weeks, the bump seemed to change from a large round bump to a long slim bump. Then, one morning in August, it was gone. There was a little stiff place, but it was barely noticeable. If Angel didn't know where it used to be, he could not have found the scar that it left.

He said, "Neesie, that bump is gone now. God made it go. Olive oil worked on bump."

Neesie said, "I know! But, I want you to keep using it until I start walking again. I am going to walk, Angel. I know now for sure. I am going to walk."

Angel said, "Angel help Neesie walk."

From that day, when the bump on her spine had completely disappeared, there was a new joy in them, a hope and a spirit of expectation. Neesie talked even more than her usual chatter and Angel began to use the word, "I" in everyday conversation.

Laura Dell was the first to notice, and she pointed it out to J. P. "Listen for the word, I, coming out of Angel's mouth. I think he's crossed a bridge that was blocked for a long time."

J. P. said, "No!"

"Oh, but yes!" Laura Dell smiled as she answered. "The baby talk is finally disappearing."

Neesie began to sing solos in church. She sang songs of power and praise. Always, Angel would push her to the front of the church and stand behind her as she sang. She never really needed him to push her chair, but it seemed like there was a spiritual strength formed between them.

There was an honesty in her voice. She never, ever performed. She just sang the songs. Many times it was the old hymns. One Sunday morning, as a distant thunderstorm rumbled past, she sang He Leadeth Me.

There was no sermon that day, because the alter was filled with people who were praying, calling out to God. Their prayers were private and the preacher didn't lay hands on anyone. There was no need for intercession because the connection was already made. His sermon could wait a week.

While Neesie blossomed, singing and smiling and talking, Angel taught himself how to juggle and dance. Every evening, for at least an hour, he was in the back room with Shady. She learned to jump rope with him. She could catch the juggling balls from across the room or pop them right back to him with her nose from up close. When Angel would finish his workout and yell, "Adriannne! Adriannne!," Shady would howl.

As the Summer came to a close, the two children continued to share their secret that Neesie was going to walk.

Neesie got a new wheelchair before school started. It was lighter and more compact with broader wheels for her to grip. Still, Angel pushed her much of the time. When he wasn't behind her chair, he was beside her.

The principal at the middle school was notified of their disabilities and their special relationship. When school started, they had matching schedules.

Cedar Ridge Middle School and Cedar Ridge High School are on the same piece of property. There is a wide lane between the buildings where the school buses come in and park. To the right of the lane is the high school and to the left is the middle school. When the students finish the eighth grade, they move across the lane into the high school for the next four years of their education.

This was the first year that Neesie and Angel had to change classrooms every period, but they found their rooms without any trouble. Some students stared at them as they went along the halls during the day, but there were also classmates from Easy Creek who already knew them. These students were at ease with them and by the second week, not many people paid them much attention.

Making new friends wasn't very easy. Neesie was in a wheelchair, of course, and Angel was obviously different. Together they were a couple that made the students who didn't know them uncomfortable. At lunch, they sat at a table by themselves. This was not their choice. Nobody wanted to sit with them. Angel could tell that Neesie's heart was breaking. She loved people so much, and she wanted to have a thousand friends. He didn't know what to do. His limited way of talking didn't help at all. For the first time in his life, he felt like a misfit. He secretly wondered if the other students would talk to Neesie if he wasn't there.

It was almost a month into the school year when they made their first new friend. He was a stocky, tanned boy who didn't talk much. One day at lunch, he came and sat down across the table from Angel and said, "Hi. My name is Bomains." He reached across the table and shook hands with Angel.

Angel said, "My name is Angel. This is Neesie."

Neesie said, "Hello. What did you say your name is?"

"Bomains. Bomains Grammercy."

Neesie smiled and said, "I've never heard a name like that."

Bomains smiled back and said, "My daddy told me that it means big hands." He held out his hands and showed them to Neesie and Angel. "But, I have small hands. And my ears are little, too."

Neesie said, "Yes, they are."

Angel said, "Yeah."

Bomains said, "Sometimes they make fun of my name and sometimes they make fun of my ears, but I don't care."

Neesie said, "We won't make fun of you."

Angel said, "We make friends."

After that, Bomains came and sat with them every day, and he and Angel ate while Neesie talked. He was a quiet boy, but his friendship was immediately accepted by both Angel and Neesie.

Bomains never acted like they were different in his eyes, and it only takes one new friend to make children feel like they fit in. On occasion, other students would sit and eat with them, which always made Neesie happy, but the everyday occupants of their lunch table were Neesie, Angel, and Bomains. That was enough.

Chapter Twenty Six

BOMAINS WAS A STUDENT OF literature and the English language. With Angel's mathematical talent and Neesie's love for people, they helped each other to make excellent grades. Their instructors were surprised and well pleased. The unlikely trio lived within physical and mental barriers because they could not find a way past them, but they presented themselves with dignity and a graceful strength. None of them complained or did anything to draw attention to themselves.

During the next few Summers, Bomains came over to the Higgins house and helped with the garden. Since he and Angel were friends, Angel helped Bomains. He had never shown interest in the garden before, but during those years, the two boys could be found there.

Angel was insistent that the rows had to be perfectly spaced and straight. The fertilizer had to be measured for each plant. To grab a small handful and toss it into a row was not permitted. Bomains, who was as patient as he was quiet, worked side by side with Angel. He was a natural teacher, and he had a basic knowledge of how to keep a garden. Most days, when Angel would go to Neesie's house to give her an afternoon massage, Bomains stayed and worked in the garden. Between Bomains, J. P., Boots, and the families, the garden grew to ten acres during the next couple of years.

Angel grew tall and slim. He wore loose fitting clothes which made him look skinny, but he was very strong. By the time he turned fifteen, he was nearly six feet tall.

Neesie grew to become a beautiful young lady. Her shiny blonde hair fell down to the middle of her back and she kept it well brushed. Her teeth were perfect and white. Her blue eyes were so clear, and shined so brightly, that it looked like a light was coming out of them. To some of her fellow students, the wheelchair appeared as a throne, because if ever a school had a queen, then Neesie Daws was the queen of Cedar Ridge Middle School. The students didn't know how much Neesie hated the wheelchair, how she wanted to stand up and walk away from it and never see it again.

Bomains, brown skinned and quiet, soon developed the muscles and the nature of a man. His hands were busy with work. His conversations were mostly of the things that needed to be accomplished next. Sometimes, he recited poetry or told stories to Angel and Neesie. He had a few favorite myths, ancient tales and songs that he loved. He sang Barbry Allen many times. His beautiful soft voice could make the story come to life. His sad eyes made his two friends understand why the rose, the flower of romantic love, was wrapped in a brier.

It is during the teen years, when childhood loses its grip, when adulthood calls from a distance, that we make our first important decisions. Life does not check to see who is happy where they are. The years do not ask if children are ready to grow. It is natural that things start happening. Rivalry becomes the little brother of friendship, and suspicion hangs around with trust, always whispering and watching.

Every step is unsure. Every dream is in danger of being killed.

At the end of the school year, when the three friends were looking forward to being sophomores, not just freshmen, in real high school, life changed suddenly.

The captain of the Cedar Ridge High School football team asked Bomains if he would like to try out for the varsity team. Bomains, excited to be a part of something, accepted the invitation with great joy. He looked forward to having new friends, not only friends, but teammates. He had only played backyard football. He knew that learning to play real football would be a challenge, but he was certain he could find a place on the team.

When he told Neesie he was going to play football, she said, "You better not."

Shocked, Bomains said, "Why not? I think I'm good enough. There's boys on the team that are a whole lot smaller than me."

"Oh, you have the size and the talent to play. If you had started playing when you were ten years old, you might be a great athlete now. But now you're not an athlete. You're a story teller and a singer."

Angel said, "Yeah."

Bomains glanced at Angel, and then he stared at Neesie in disbelief. "I can't believe you! For four years, it has been just us, you and Angel and me. We were left out of everything. Now, I finally get a chance to be included in something and you don't want me to go. Come on, Neesie. I know Angel doesn't understand how much this means, but you should."

Neesie, her face showing how deeply she was hurt, said, "Bomains, Angel and I never left you out of anything. Her voice cracked and her eyes filled with tears as she said, "We never...."

Angel said, "Yeah."

Bomains said, "Angel, will you shut..." He bit off any more words for a few seconds. Then he tried to tell them again how important his opportunity was, but the words that came out of his heart through his mouth were not about football. "Y'all are my friends. You will always be my friends, and I love you both." Tears rolled down his cheeks. "But I can do something that y'all can't do. I want to play football. I want to be on a team. I want to see how strong I am. I want to hear a crowd cheering for me. Nobody even notices me. Nobody knows who I am. I want to change that."

Neesie looked directly into Bomains' eyes and said, "Okay, Bomains, go ahead and play football. We hope you become a star on the team. Just remember, we're your friends. You're never left out as far as we are concerned. So, give me a hug and shake Angel's hand. We can go in different directions, but our hearts are bound together like roses and briers."

Angel said, "Yeah."

Bomains did shake hands with Angel, and he gave Neesie a hug and a kiss on the cheek, which he had never done before.

He walked away with his head down. He looked more like a lost puppy than an athlete. Neesie said, "Lord, look after our friend and protect him."

Angel said, "In Jesus, amen."

Neesie whispered, "Amen."

Chapter Twenty Seven

BOMAINS CAME TO HELP IN the garden a few more times after school was out for summer, but the amount of time between his visits grew longer. Everyone, including Bomains, knew that his time in the garden at Easy Creek was over.

A sadness fell over the Higgins and Daws families that year. A new war was unfolding. And Boots was forced to decide whether to retire or re-enlist for four more years. Although Rachel wanted him to stop being a soldier, she didn't pressure him about his decision. Neesie was openly against her daddy going away again. She asked him several times if a child that he had never met was more important than his own daughter.

Boots said, "Sweetheart, I know that you're here at home safe. There are people who are being murdered by evil men."

Neesie had an answer ready for his explanation. "If you get killed by those evil men, who will protect Mommy and me? Why have so many of our good men died for other men's children? Who did the last war help, and the one before that?"

Boots didn't have an answer and it bothered him because he didn't.

One late summer evening, J. P. saw Boots walking in the garden. It had been a bad year for growing things. The Spring had been too cool, and the Summer was too dry. Most of the produce had been small or covered in bad spots. The families lost money. When Bomains stopped showing up to help, Angel began to ride his bicycle again. Hours at a time, he would pedal around the yard, around and around and around.

J. P. came out to talk with Boots. They walked to the picnic area at the corner of the property. They sat beside the creek as the day faded. Mourning doves cooed their last good nights to each other and the stars began to show themselves.

J. P. sat without speaking until Boots began to talk. "I have made my decision," he said. The statement was solid and final. "I have fought against and killed people in three different places on this earth. I have gone where my government sent me and I have attacked who they told me to attack. I have held eighteen year old boys in my arms, some who were burned beyond recognition, and watched their breath stop. I have felt the moment when their hearts stopped beating."

Boots looked up at the darkening sky. "I can't justify a single death on either side."

J. P. said, "You were fighting for the helpless. You were fighting for their freedom and ours."

Boots didn't say a word in response.

After a long, long silence, J. P. stated the obvious answer. "Nobody you thought you were fighting to help is any better off, are they?"

Boots shook his head.

"None of them are free now, are they?"

Boots shook his head again. "No."

J. P. said, "So, I take it that you are going to retire."

Boots straightened up in his chair. "I am. And then I am going to live the rest of my life as a free citizen. I..... will be free."

The Daws family were happy with the decision Boots made and so were the Higgins. They all had a big picnic beside Easy Creek on Labor Day weekend as the long, sad summer came to a close.

Boots seemed to be tense, like he had been the month before he re-enlisted four years ago. But this anxiousness wasn't caused by his decision. He didn't know what he was going to do next week. For twenty four years, he had been a soldier. Before that, he was a teenager. Tomorrow wouldn't be a war, but it was definitely going to be an adventure. His daughter sat next to him in her wheelchair, holding his hand and smiling a truly happy smile. "You're finally home, Daddy. Every night and every morning, you're home."

What Neesie said, what his beautiful little wheelchair bound daughter said, reminded him of one certain truth. Of all the people in the world, there was one man who was finally free. Boots Daws was free.

The summer was gone, and Neesie and Angel began their sophomore year of high school. Surprisingly, the classes didn't seem overly difficult. Their interaction with each other and Bomains had created a solid foundation of knowledge to draw from as they learned. Their study habits were good.

The other students bustled around them, dodging Neesie's wheelchair and ignoring her guardian, Angel, who walked faithfully beside or behind her along the halls of education.

Bomains was in some of their classes, of course, and he would always give them a friendly hello and a smile when he saw them. But during lunch he sat with the athletes. When he would enter the lunchroom, those players who were already seated would give a cheer of, "Bomains!"

The rowdy salute made Bomains grin and wave to their table. He was hearing his name. He was being recognized. He had come out of the dark corner into the light and the other students could actually see him. He was part of the team.

In the real world, on the football field, Bomains wasn't a very good player. He was years behind in technique. His footwork was slow which made him easy to block. He didn't know how to tackle at all and he wasn't fast enough to carry the ball.

In the weight room he was a beast, out lifting most of the other players and growing stronger every week. The coaches had hopes of turning him into a linebacker, but so far he was a boy who could lift a lot of weight and that was all he was.

No new friend came to take the empty place Bomains had left. Neesie began to feel isolated. Angel sensed that she was lonely. One day, as they were finishing their lunch, Angel said, "Neesie, if you want, tomorrow, Angel sit somewhere else. Maybe... maybe some new friends come sit here."

Neesie looked at Angel, a great fear in her eyes, "Angel, what if nobody does? What if nobody comes to sit with me, and somebody comes to sit with you?"

"Me come back to you and I bring them with me."

Neesie asked, "And what if some people come to sit with me, but nobody comes to sit with you? Oh, Angel, I couldn't stand that! I would shoo them away and demand that you come back to me."

Angel said, "Yeah, me too. Angel come back. Angel always come back." And then he smiled his little half smile and Neesie laughed.

That day, the possible solution to their separation from the other students at lunchtime was considered, talked about, and rejected. They were together, and maybe some day, Bomains would come back to sit at their table again.

Chapter Twenty Eight

FOOTBALL SEASON ENDED IN NOVEMBER. Bomains looked magnificent in his uniform, but he didn't get to play very much. The team won as many as they lost and the coaches hoped for a better season next year. The quarterback, Ace Kyker, had played very well and next year he would be a senior. Plus, if the young linebacker, Bomains, could learn to play a little better, the defense should be tough.

In January, Neesie and Angel got a surprise. One night it snowed. Not a serious snow, but there must have been at least three inches on the ground. Angel rushed to Neesie's house that morning. Rachel dressed her in warm clothes and wrapped her in a blanket. Angel pushed the wheelchair out into the yard and spun it around and around while Neesie waved her arms above her head and cheered.

After about twenty minutes of rolling around in the snow, Neesie said, "Let's go in and sit by the window and drink hot chocolate. I have something to tell you."

Angel said, "Okay."

When they came in through the kitchen door, Rachel stopped them. She put a large towel down and Angel dried his shoes and then he dried the wheelchair off, wiping the floor as dry as possible as well. They went into the living room and sat beside a window, looking out across the snow covered yard.

Rachel brought cups of hot chocolate and they sat and blew across the tops of their cups, trying to cool it so they wouldn't burn their tongues when they sipped.

Neesie said, "That was fun, wasn't it?"

Angel said, "Yeah."

Neesie grabbed Angel's hand and made him lean over close so she could whisper in his ear. "Do you want to know why I wanted to come inside, Angel?"

Angel looked at her face from the corner of his eye, "No, but I guess."

Smiling a great big smile, Neesie said, "Okay, guess."

"Last night I dream that your wheelchair turned over and you get hurt. You want to come in because you afraid Angel turn you over in the snow."

Neesie whispered, "No, Angel. Playing in the snow was fun!" She leaned even closer, put her lips against his ear. "I wanted to come in because my feet were getting cold."

Angel said, "Oh."

Neesie raised her hand and it looked like she was going to slap him.

Angel's eyes suddenly opened wide. Just as he was about to speak, Neesie clamped her hand over his mouth. He spoke a muffled "Ohhhh!"

"Hush, Angel! Hush!" She whispered, holding a firm grip.

Angel gave a quick nod. Neesie turned loose of his jaw. In an excited whisper, he asked, "Neesie, you feel your feet?"

"Yes, and I can move them a little bit, too!"

Angel stood up, sat back down and looked around. "Who we tell?"

"Nobody. If we tell Mommy, she'll take me to the doctor and they'll want to operate on me. I want to see if I can get well on my own."

Angel said, "You get well, Neesie. You get well in olive oil. You get well in Jesus. Amen."

Neesie said, "Amen. Now, here's what I think we should do. After you massage my legs and back, I want you to bend my legs. I will try to push back when you bend them. That way we can see if some strength is coming back with the feeling."

Angel put his hand on Neesie's arm. "Neesie will walk," he whispered. "Angel help Neesie walk in Jesus!"

Neesie put her head against Angel's shoulder. "I know you will, Angel."

They looked out at the snow and sipped their warm drinks. Although it was winter, although they seemed to be two young people forced aside by life's cruel circumstance, they were full of hope. Suddenly, a miracle was possible.

The snow melted quickly and left a cold muddy covering over everything for a few days. But to Neesie and Angel, it seemed like Springtime had already arrived. Neesie blossomed with new beauty. Her body was taking on the shape of a lady and she wore a constant, sincere smile.

Angel seemed to stand taller. His shoulders seemed broader. His hands held firmly to everything he touched.

Their secret was their strength, and for both of them, their new strength was impossible to conceal. They were always looking at everything as if it was brand new. They leaned in and talked quietly at lunch, seeming to be in a world of their own. Everything they did had the appearance of young love. Few of the other students were surprised and not many of them cared.

Neesie, as beautiful as she looked, was still confined to a wheelchair. Angel was so dedicated to her that he probably never noticed anyone else.

As Winter faded and the warm sunshine of Spring came again, there was one student who did notice Neesie's beauty. Ace Kyker thought she was the prettiest girl in the world. He wanted to ask her for a date. He wanted to touch her hair, to kiss her and tell her how beautiful she was. He wanted to tell her that he would take care of her, not Angel. He wanted to move Angel out of the way, far away.

Ace wanted to get Angel out of Cedar Ridge High

School. Since Ace was a junior, he needed to do it soon. There was only one year left for him to win her heart.

It was during April, when the football team has Spring Training, that Ace found his chance. During this time, the team has its annual hazing week. Since Bomains had joined the team after Spring Training the year before, he was considered a first year player who could be hazed.

One day after lunch, Ace and several other players stopped Bomains as he came out of the lunchroom. Ace said, "Hey, Bomains, don't you know that crippled girl and her stupid freak that follows her around?"

Immediately, Bomains' heart began to race. He thought the players were going to make fun of him because he was friends with Neesie and Angel. "Yes, they are my friends, why?"

Ace said, "I know why you're friends with them. You like that cripple girl, don't you?"

Bomains said, "Yeah, she's a nice girl. Like I said, she's my friend."

"Oh, no, she's not your friend. You're in love with her, aren't you?"

"No, she's...."

"You want to marry her, don't you, Bomains?"

At that moment, Neesie came out of the lunchroom door. Angel was pushing her along. Bomains jumped and blushed as they came out.

Ace grinned with only his teeth. "See there, boys, I was right. Bomains loves the cripple girl. Well, I think you need to propose to her."

Bomains looked at Ace, confused and embarrassed. "What? No!"

Ace stepped towards Bomains and the other players followed his lead. "Oh, you have to, rookie. You have to do what the other players say."

Bomains said, "I can't. I can't do that."

Angel had stopped. Neesie was now hearing every word of the conversation.

Ace said, "Go ahead, Bomains. You know you want to, anyway. Go over there and get down on one knee and ask her to marry you."

Bomains was trapped. If he didn't do what he was told, he would be kicked off of the football team. He took three short steps towards Neesie and Ace got just what he wanted.

Angel stepped between Bomains and Neesie. "No! Bomains, you not bother Neesie! Neesie your friend."

A crowd of students began to gather.

Ace said, "Do it, Bomains. Don't let that dummy stop you. You're a linebacker for crying out loud."

Neesie, panicking, began to cry.

Again, Angel said, "Bomains, you not!" Bomains hesitated.

Ace gave his order. "If he tries to stop you from proposing, you whip his butt, Bomains!" The other players cheered their encouragement for Bomains.

Angel gave one final warning. "Bomains, you not! Angel is fast! Bomains lose!"

This brought a loud round of threats from the football

players. Bomains took a step forward and swung a long arcing fist at Angel.

So fast that nobody could see him move, Angel bobbed his head and hit Bomains in the middle of his forehead with just the palm of his hand. "Bomains, you not!"

Neesie said, "Bomains, please stop. You're going to get hurt."

Ace said, "Don't let that cripple girl keep you from playing football, Bomains. Beat his butt."

Bomains swung again and missed. Angel said, "Bomains, you not hurt Neesie!"

Bomains stepped forward and swung as hard as he could. By now, he knew what was going to happen, but he couldn't see a way out. His fist never touched anything. He felt Angel's counter punch, and he sat down on his butt, stunned. Blood was pouring from his nose.

His teammates were yelling at him to get up. Ace was yelling the loudest. Bomains stood up and staggered back a couple of steps. Then he charged straight at Angel. Angel sidestepped and Bomains ran headfirst into Neesie's wheelchair, knocking it over backwards. The students watching screamed in horror.

Angel, seeing Neesie's head snap back when the chair hit the ground, became enraged. He grabbed Bomains and lifted him over his shoulder and slammed him to the pavement. Bomains had the breath knocked out of him and couldn't move. Ace and the other football players charged at Angel, swinging their fists and cursing.

But Angel stood his ground, and the players' heads were snapping back at a rapid pace. Every time one of them came within reach, Angel struck. He hit hard, black eye hard, mouth busting hard, rib crushing hard.

Finally, they almost had him down, but Bomains had caught his breath. Instead of going after Angel, he lunged for Ace. He wrapped his forearm under Ace's chin and squeezed. Within a few seconds, Ace's whole body went limp, and Bomains dropped him to the ground. He turned just in time to see Angel hit a player with an uppercut and then, in one fluid move, spin and elbow the last standing player in the temple. Both of them staggered backwards, stunned.

Angel followed them with his fists raised. Bomains stepped between them and shouted, "Angel, stop! Angel, it's me! Stop!"

Angel shouted, "Bomains, you not!"

"Okay, Angel, I won't. I promise you, I won't. Just stop, okay? Stop! I'm your friend, Angel. Please! Stop!"

Slowly, the rage cleared from Angel's eyes, and then, "Neesie! Neesie! Where Neesie? Neesie got hurt! Angel help Neesie!"

Neesie still lay on her back in the overturned wheelchair. Angel and Bomains ran to her, kneeled down on each side of her. Several girls were comforting her, trying to keep her from fainting. When Angel spoke to her, she calmed immediately.

"Angel, did they hurt you?"

"No, Angel is okay. Is Neesie hurt?"

"I don't think so. I hit my head a little, but I think I'm alright."

Angel and Bomains raised the wheelchair back on to its wheels. A couple of the girls held Neesie's hands and straightened her hair. Angel said, "Neesie isn't hurt?"

"No, I'm not hurt at all."

Angel said, "I told you I dreamed, but you not hurt. You not hurt in Jesus. Amen."

Neesie and Bomains both said, "Amen."

When they looked up from checking on Neesie, the principal and the football coach were walking up and asking what had happened.

Ace said, "Bomains spoke to Neesie and her dummy went crazy and started trying to beat everybody up. It's a good thing I came along and broke it up. My boys here were having a hard time protecting everybody."

Bomains turned to face Ace and shouted, "You liar! Angel was the only one who tried to stop it. You were egging it on from the beginning. You caused the whole thing. You lying punk! If you get Angel in trouble, I'll whip you every day until you confess that this was your fault."

The principal stood still for a minute with his hand on his chin. Finally, he said, "I want everybody to go to the school nurse's office. I'm going to my office and call every parent of every student that's involved. Coach, you go with them and don't let anything else start."

The coach said, "Yes, sir," and he started to walk away with all of them. Angel was pushing Neesie and Bomains was walking beside Angel.

Suddenly, the principal called, "Hey, Coach!"

The coach turned and looked back.

"You don't need to say a word to your players or any of the students, you understand?"

The coach nodded.

"Not one word, Coach!"

The coach cringed and nodded again.

Several students were hurt and everybody was in trouble.

Chapter Twenty Nine

AFTER THE NURSE CHECKED THE students out, she sent two of the football players to the doctor's office for a couple of stitches. Angel's punches had been solid. The boys were lucky that Bomains was able to stop him.

The principal brought Neesie, Ace, Bomains, Angel, and one other football player into his office. He said, "Now, before everyone's parents get here, I want to hear what happened, and somebody better be telling me the truth." He looked at all five of the students.

The football player had one eye that was swelling shut. He shook his head, not wanting to talk. He was confused and his head was hurting so bad that he couldn't think clearly. Anyway, he didn't really know what had happened. A silly joke turned into a brawl and Neesie's chair was turned over, which was awful. He was embarrassed. He wanted to apologize, but he didn't want Ace to get into trouble. He wanted to run out of the office, but he couldn't do that.

Bomains said, "I'll tell you what happened, and I am willing to accept whatever punishment I have coming. I will tell the truth, Sir."

The Principal said, "Okay, let's hear it."

"I was being hazed by Ace and the other players. He wanted me to get down on one knee and pretend I was asking Neesie to marry me. I didn't want to, but he said that he knew I was in love with that cripple girl and he insisted. I didn't want to get kicked off of the team, so I was going to do it. Angel tried to stop me, because it was scaring Neesie and she was crying. I should have said no, but Ace and the other players said if her dummy tried to stop me, I should whip his butt."

The principal said, "Wait a minute. Who called Angel a dummy?"

Bomains said, "Ace did. I would never. Angel is my best friend. And Neesie shouldn't be called a cripple, either."

The principal said, "Go ahead."

"Okay, so Angel stood between me and Neesie. Ace and them were yelling at me to hit him and I took a swing and missed. He didn't really hit me back until I swung the third time. He was telling me to stop, but they were yelling at me to hit him and I couldn't. He was too fast. After the third swing, he hit me and busted my nose. I deserved it. Then I ran at him and tried to tackle him, but he disappeared. I guess he sidestepped or something. That's when I ran into Neesie's chair and knocked her over, and I am so sorry, Neesie."

Neesie said, "It's alright, Bomains. I'm not hurt."

Bomains continued, "Anyway, Angel thought Neesie was hurt and you know what happened then. He picked me up like I was a feather and slammed me down. It knocked the breath out of me. While I was trying to catch my breath, Ace and the other boys ganged up on Angel. The fight between me and Angel was over. I lost and they didn't have any reason to jump on Angel."

The principal asked, "So, the fight started between you and Angel?"

"Yes, sir."

"Then, how did two other boys get sent to the doctor for stitches and another one's sitting here with a swelled up eye?"

Ace said, "That's what I tried to tell you."

Bomains said, "Shut up, Ace." Ace stopped talking.

The principal said, "You'll get your chance to talk, Ace. Go ahead, Bomains."

"They all ganged up on Angel, but he is so fast! He was mad, too! Anyway, they almost had him down when I got my breath back. I grabbed Ace and pulled him out of the way. I choked him until he fell, and then I went to help Angel, but he didn't need any help. The boys that were beating him up did. They were trying to get away because Angel was about to kill them. I got in front of Angel and when he saw it was me, he stopped fighting. So, I started the fight because I wanted to play football. I lost the fight because I can't fight very well, and I stopped the fight because Angel knows that I'm his friend. It was me. I made a wrong decision. I should never have bothered Neesie and Angel should have beat me up a lot worse than he did. He tried to avoid getting into a fight. Angel, I promise you. I will always be your friend. I was wrong. I was so wrong."

Angel said, "Okay."

The principal turned to Ace. "Ace, what part of that story isn't true? And remember, everybody else is going to tell their version as well."

Ace said, "Why should I say anything? I already know that you're going to believe Bomains. He ain't nothing but a clumsy goofball, anyway. Everybody laughs at him behind his back. Look what happened. He got in a fight with a dummy, but all he was able to do was knock that little cripple girl's wheelchair over. The only reason he choked me out was because he jumped me from behind."

The principal clenched his jaw and shook his head. "Young man."

Laura Dell and Rachel came rushing into the principal's office. They stopped and stared at Neesie and Angel, who both seemed to be unharmed. When Laura Dell saw the swelling of Bomains' nose, she gasped. "Bomains, are you hurt very bad?"

Bomains said, "Not as bad as I should be. It was my fault, Mrs. Higgins. Angel didn't do anything wrong."

The two ladies looked at the other boys. One of them had a very swelled black eye and the other one had a very red face.

The principal said, "Mrs. Higgins, Mrs. Daws, let's wait until the other parents get here and I think we can sort this mess out. A couple of boys had to go to the doctor for stitches, but nobody was very seriously hurt."

Rachel said, "Stitches?"

Laura Dell said, "Angel, what did you do?"

At the same time, Neesie and Bomains said, "It wasn't his fault!"

When all of the parents had arrived, the principal escorted everyone to the auditorium. The students returned from the doctor's office, one with a bandage over his eye and the other with a stitch in his lip covered by a band aid.

There were fourteen parents, seven students, a football coach, and the principal in the auditorium. They weren't all spread out at all, but gathered into one corner. They waited for an explanation of how a brawl had started outside of the lunchroom.

The principal told the story of what had happened as Bomains had told him. He asked the other boys if they had anything they wanted to change about the story. Only one of them said, "If somebody's a karate expert, they're supposed to warn you before they get into a fight. That's the law."

Boots Daws laughed out loud. J. P. looked at the floor, his hands over his face. He secretly wondered if Angel had yelled, "Adriane," after the fight was over.

Mr. and Mrs. Kyker were looking at their son as if he was a stranger.

The principal asked, "Does anyone want to get the police involved? Does anyone want to prefer charges?" There were a few head shakes and a few blank stares. "I am glad. Here's what I want to do. All of you except Neesie get a three day, in school suspension. You will do your regular classwork. You will not talk. You will not argue. You will not act up in any way. You will all be in the same room for the entire three days. After that, you will go back to your regular classes. I don't want to hear one negative word about any of you for the rest of the year. Do y'all understand?"

The boys all mumbled, "Yes, sir."

The principal turned to the football coach and asked, "Coach, do you have anything to add?"

The coach said, "Bomains, you're off the team."

Bomains didn't respond to the coach, but he looked at Neesie and winked.

As they were all walking back to their cars, Ace's father asked J. P., "What's this about Angel being a karate expert?"

J. P. replied, "I don't know. That was the first I heard of it, too." He turned his back to Mr. Kyker and walked away.

Chapter Thirty

BOMAINS SAT NEXT TO ANGEL during the in school suspension days. Although Angel was tense, he didn't have
any episodes of bad behavior. Ace looked at Bomains a
few times as if he wanted to talk, but Bomains always gave
him a quick head shake. He didn't want to talk to Ace.

The two girls who helped Neesie when her chair was
turned over sat with her during lunch so she wouldn't
be alone. Her friendly nature won their hearts and they
became friends. She missed Angel terribly. During class
there were several times that she felt hot tears welling up
in her eyes.

As soon as the last class of every day was over, they
found each other and rode home together in Rachel's car.
Neesie would talk about what happened during the day
and what people said about the fight and how everyone
was mad at Ace except the football team. Every once in
a while, she would ask Angel a question and he would
usually say, "Yeah," and she would start talking again.

One subject they could not talk about on the way home was how Neesie's legs and back were gaining strength. They went straight to Neesie's massage bed as soon as they got to her house. Angel rubbed her legs, back, and shoulders before he put olive oil on his hands and gently massaged her lower back and legs. Then Neesie would lie on her back and Angel would push against the bottoms of her feet. Ever so slightly, every day, Angel could feel her pushing harder against his hands with her legs.

The massage time was like a secret life for them. Neesie constantly reminded Angel that he must not tell anyone that she had feeling and strength in her legs. She was afraid that her mother would take her to the doctor and he would want to do surgery. She was absolutely not willing to have any other treatment than Angel's massages and olive oil.

As the school year was ending, the school faculty decided to have a talent show. There wouldn't be an actual contest, just a night for the students to perform and show what they did away from school. To Neesie's surprise, Angel signed up as an act for the show. She said, "Angel, what are you going to do?"

He said, "Juggle dance."

"Oh, like you did that day at the house?"

"No, something new with Shady. Do you want to see me dance with Shady? She helps Angel juggle dance now. All the time in my dance room, we juggle dance."

Neesie said, "I would love to see it. Can I come into your dance room?"

Until that day, no one had been invited into Angel's back room. Laura Dell and J. P. had noticed that a different tune was being played quite often. It was John Anderson's I'm Just an Old Chunk of Coal.

Angel asked Neesie, "You not tell nobody?"

"No, of course I won't tell. It will be one of our secrets."

Angel said, "Okay."

One Saturday morning, Angel, Shady and Neesie came through the living room and went into Angel's dance room. There was no explanation or grand announcement. Laura Dell and J. P. were sitting on the couch and they watched them pass by. They looked at each other with an unasked question it their eyes.

Even though they seldom spied on Angel, because much of his world was separated from other people, they slipped down the hall to listen just outside of the closed door to the room.

Angel said, "First, Angel has to put on dance outfit."

There were a few minutes of silence as Angel dressed for his part. He had on pants that were too short, a dress jacket that fit well across the chest, but the sleeves didn't reach his wrists, and a pair of old dress shoes. On top of his head was a beat up old felt hat.

"Angel looks like a hobo?" he asked Neesie. She nodded and smiled. He handed her a piece of paper and said, "Now, I walk back there and you read this loud like announcer and push button here to turn on music, okay?"

Neesie said, "Okay. Will Shady start with you?"

"Yeah, she dance with me and help with juggle dance. Ready?"

Neesie nodded and Angel and Shady walked to the far wall of the room. He took a deep breath and said, "Okay, you read paper like announcer."

Neesie held the paper up and read, "Ladiessss annnnd gentlemennnn, presenting Michael Angelo and his dancing dogggg Ladyyyy Nightshade!"

She pressed the play button and the intro music started, followed by John Anderson's voice singing "I'm just an old chunk of coal..."

Angel strutted along the floor as Shady criss-crossed between his steps, perfectly in time. He spun and stepped around in a modified soft shoe style. His long legs and arms, combined with the undersized clothes, made him look graceful and out of balance at the same time. After the first verse, he pulled a black juggling ball out of the jacket pocket and held it up for Neesie to see.

Under her breath, Neesie said, "Uh oh, here we go!"

Angel bounced the ball off of the floor and Shady popped it back to him with her nose. As soon as he caught it, there was another ball bouncing to Shady, and she bounced it off of her nose. Then the third ball was in the air and the juggle dance started.

Neesie's eyes couldn't keep up with Angel and Shady as they danced around the room. Angel whirled and stepped as the black balls seemed to know where they were supposed to go. The arc of flying balls whirled over his shoulder as he turned. He never missed a step as he caught them and pitched them high and wide so Shady could jump through them twice with two quick hops. She yipped in joy as Angel bounced one out of the circle of whirling balls, and she popped it back into the circle perfectly. But, now there was an extra ball in the whirling arc, a shining, clear one. It looked like a large diamond!

As the final instrumental run was played out, Angel and Shady danced around while he made the three original balls disappear into his jacket pocket. Then, as the music faded, he strutted back to the far wall, tossing the diamond ball into the air, walking along like a hobo without a care in this world. Shady trotted along beside him. She knew without a doubt that she and Angel were definitely the "Rage of the Age."

Angel walked back to Neesie and said, "We do juggle dance, me and Shady."

Neesie said, "Angel! That was amazing! You are a diamond already! Oh, I can't wait to see you on the stage dancing."

Angel said, "I change clothes. We go sit in sunshine this morning, okay? We go sit at picnic place."

Laura Dell and J. P. scurried back to the couch. In a few minutes, Angel appeared, pushing a grinning Neesie along in front of him. He said, "Papa, we go to picnic area for a while."

J. P. said, "Alright, Son. Y'all watch for snakes."

Laura Dell said, "Bye, kids."

Both Neesie and Angel said, "Bye," and waved as they went out the door. Shady trotted along in front of them.

Chapter Thirty One

AFTER THE THREE DAY SUSPENSION, Bomains found himself without any friends. He sat by himself during lunch at a table in the farthest corner of the lunchroom. Nobody saluted him with a rowdy call of his name anymore. He was alone, but he didn't feel pity for himself. He had done an awful thing. He had betrayed his two best friends in hopes that he would become somebody special on the football field. He had humiliated himself.

Bomains believed he could strengthen his character by sitting alone for the rest of the school year. In his mind, he needed to watch people, to see who they really were and what they were like so he could figure out who he was and how he should try to fit in as his life unfolded. He understood that Neesie and Angel were his very good friends, but he also understood that he had not been a good friend to them. He couldn't explain to himself why he had let himself be goaded into fighting Angel.

One day, he came to Neesie and Angel's table, humble and apologetic. Neesie asked him to sit down in his usual seat, but he shook his head.

"Not this year, Neesie," he said. "Maybe next year, but I don't deserve to sit with y'all right now. He gave Neesie a quick hug and patted Angel on the shoulder. One more time, he apologized. "I am so sorry for how I acted. I will never do anything like that again to you or anybody else."

Neesie said, "It's alright, Bomains. Please sit down."

Angel said, "Yeah. We friends, Bomains."

Bomains shook his head and walked to his seat in the corner. He wasn't ready to come out of his self imposed exile.

One day, as he was coming out of the lunchroom, Ace came up to him and said, "Bomains, I need to talk to you."

"No, you don't."

Ace walked along beside him. "Look, I have been talking to Coach. I believe he will let you back on the team if you go and ask him."

Bomains looked away from Ace. He couldn't stand the sight of him. "I don't want back on the team, Ace."

"Sure you do. With the team we have coming back, we can win the district. You'll be the captain of the defense, Bomains. We might go undefeated."

Bomains said, "No. Now, leave me alone." He walked faster and turned away from Ace. Ace stopped and watched him walk away.

The talent show was scheduled for a Thursday night. The next Monday would be the graduation ceremonies, so there wasn't a conflict in the schedule. The principal was going to be the Master of Ceremonies, so the acts couldn't be too rowdy. Everyone who signed up was expected to be on stage at least three minutes and not more than five.

There were comedy acts, skits with several students on stage, a Shakespeare recital, ballet, and a band of teenagers who called themselves The Garage Band. All together, there were sixteen acts, so the show would last almost two hours. Neesie had let the principal know that Angel must be the final act. She demanded it, and the principal had laughed at how serious she was and agreed immediately. She also gave him a piece of paper with the exact words to use when he introduced Angel. The principal, knowing how important minor details could be to autistic children, put the paper in his shirt pocket and promised to read it when Angel's turn to perform came.

The night of the talent show finally arrived. Angel's family and Neesie's family were all sitting together in one group. Bomains was sitting a few seats away. Boots motioned for him to come and sit with them, but Bomains looked at the floor and shook his head, no. Boots stood up and walked over to Bomains and said, "You get your tail over there where you belong. And if you don't sit right at the end of the row next to my daughter, you're going to have to deal with me after the show."

Bomains went and sat where Boots told him to sit. Neesie looked at him and smiled. Laura Dell was sitting beside him in the next seat. She leaned over and said, "You can't undo it, Sweetheart."

He looked at her with a deep sadness in his eyes. "I want to. I want to make it so it never happened. I am so ashamed of myself."

Laura Dell said, "We have all felt the way you feel. You're a good person. Put it behind you. You'll do better next time."

"Yes, Ma'am."

Laura Dell patted him on the shoulder a couple of times and to Bomains, that meant everything.

There were some talented performers in the show, and there were some who seemed silly, but they wanted to be on the stage. There are people who can walk out on a stage and feel like they have finally made it home for the first time in their lives. The quality of their first act may be poor, but they know.

Everything rolled along on schedule, maybe a little bit behind, but the students were having fun. The audience was enjoying the show. Finally, it was Angel's time.

"Ladiessss annnnd gentlemennnn, presenting Michael Angelo and his dancing dogggg Ladyyyy Nightshade!"

The music started and Angel came out strutting and dancing in his hobo outfit. John Anderson's unique voice sang, "Hey, I'm just an old chunk of coal…" Shady trotted between Angel's feet as he danced, never out of time, never out of step. When Angel pulled the first black ball out of his pocket, Neesie tapped Bomains' arm and said, "Here we go!"

And there they went! Angel was whirling, dancing, juggling. Shady stayed in perfect position, popping the balls back to Angel and jumping through the ring of whirling balls. Suddenly, the music was fading out, and Angel was strutting away to the back of the stage with Shady prissing along beside him like the queen of the dog world.

Angel tossed the diamond shaped ball into the air and caught it a couple of times as they disappeared backstage.

The music was over. There was a long pause. Total silence. And then the crowd went crazy. Ace Kyker, who was standing at the back near the door, turned to walk out, but he couldn't make himself go. Who was he kidding? That was unbelievable. Still, he didn't clap or cheer. He was too cool to do that.

When the roar of the crowd didn't die down, the principal ran backstage and told Angel, "You have to do a curtain call!"

"A what?"

"A curtain call! Come with me." He grabbed Angel by the wrist and led him back out to the front of the stage. Shady trotted along behind them. The cheering became even louder. Angel stood still, not even looking around.

The principal, above the roar, said, "Angel, you need to bow!"

Angel said, "Okay." He dropped to one knee and held both hands above his head as if signaling a touchdown.

Shady took a running start and jumped up on his shoulders. She wagged her stubby tail and yipped her appreciation to the audience.

All of the performers who were backstage came out and gathered on each side of Angel and Shady. They threw kisses and waved goodbye as the crowd finally began to file out of the auditorium.

Everyone was gone but Neesie and her family and J. P. and Laura Dell and Bomains. Angel yelled from the stage, "Angel change clothes and bring Shady. We go home, okay?"

Laura Dell laughed. J. P. called back, "We'll be right here, Son."

Bomains asked, "Should I stay a few minutes and brag on the star?"

Neesie said, "You better. He might not say anything if you don't, but just watch his face light up when he sees you."

Angel came out and put his bag of clothes in Neesie's lap. As usual, he pushed her along as they walked towards the exit doors. He said, "Neesie, you like my juggle dance tonight?"

"I sure did! That was better than when you first showed it to me."

Angel said, "We practice a lot." He looked at Bomains. "You coming home with us?"

Bomains smiled and said, "Not tonight, Angel, but maybe soon. Boy, you can really dance!"

"You sit with us at lunch again, now?"

Bomains shrugged his shoulders and said, "Sure, I guess so."

Angel said, "Okay."

Chapter Thirty Two

THAT SUMMER WAS A HOT one. Mr. Green said that it was time for him to retire. Boots bought the store from him. He decided to add some small farm equipment and supplies. This meant the store needed to be made larger, so there was construction on the lot.

Boots hired Bomains as a helper at the store. Laura Dell and Rachel worked in the garden with Angel's help sometimes. J. P. would come home from work and look around to see who was busiest and pitch in for a couple of hours in the late afternoons.

Angel worked in the garden when he wanted to. In the middle of the day, he was usually sitting in the shade with Neesie at the picnic area. One day in June, he waded out into the creek and started piling rocks in the water.

Neesie said, "Angel, what are you doing?"

"Angel...I make Neesie a place to swim. Swimming will make your legs stronger."

Neesie watched him for a few minutes, and then she said, "We're going to need a shovel and a pick. I want it to be at least four feet deep and I want a floating tube that I can slide down in so I can kick my legs and paddle around. It's going to be a beautiful swimming pool, Angel. Of course, you'll have to clean the brush away from the banks so there won't be any snakes. You can do that, can't you?"

Angel said, "Yeah." He put as many rocks as he could find along the bottom of the creek and the water level began to rise. After he had worked a couple of hours, he needed tools, so they went back to the barn and grabbed a shovel, a mattock, and a rake.

Angel ran into the house and came out with three cold drinks in a small cooler. He said, "This one for us now and one for after I work too hard on the swimming pool." Neesie held the cooler and Angel carried the tools while he pushed her along with one hand.

All through the hot afternoon, Angel dug the bottom of the creek up and shoveled the mud onto the rock dam. It wasn't a task he had done before, so he was slow and steady. By late afternoon, when the sun was falling towards the western row of trees, the water was up to Angel's waist, and he was tired.

He climbed up the bank and sat down in a chair next to Neesie. She handed him the last drink out of the cooler and said, "It's getting pretty deep. Now, we need to find a tube for me to get into. I think Daddy has some down at the store. We can call and see. Maybe, when it gets hot tomorrow, you can put me in a tube and I will be able to paddle around our little swimming pool. I think it will help my legs get stronger, don't you?"

Angel said, "Yeah, maybe the water help your legs."

Neesie said, "We're going swimming, Angel! Right here in our own little pool that we built, we are going to swim."

Angel said, "Yeah."

The next morning, Angel tried to help in the garden, but he was sore all over. He sat with Neesie in the shade of a tree in the yard as they impatiently watched the sun climb towards noon. After lunch, Angel used his bicycle pump to inflate the tube that Boots brought from the store, and they started for the picnic area.

As they were leaving, Rachel said, "Angel, how deep did you make that hole you dug?"

Angel held his hand just above his waste and said, "About here."

Rachel said, "Well, I guess that will be alright, but y'all be careful. I mean it, Neesie. Don't get yourself hurt."

Neesie said, "Don't worry, Mommy, I won't."

When they came to the picnic area, Angel looked into the pool to make sure that there were no snakes along the bank or in the water. Then, he dropped the tube into the water. It floated over against the dam and stayed. He moved Neesie's wheelchair as close to the bank as he could get it. He fixed the chair at an angle to the bank and jumped down into the pool of water. The bank was steep. There was not a step yet, so he was going to have to pull her down out of her wheelchair.

Angel stood as close to the bank as he could get while still keeping his balance. He said, "Neesie, you lean out and Angel will catch you."

Neesie was nervous and she asked, "Are you sure?"

Angel said, "Maybe, but maybe I drop you."

"Well, if you do, you better pick me up!" And then she leaned out and fell into Angel's arms. She locked her arms around his neck and shoulders as he reached for the tube and pulled it over next to them. He groaned as he raised her up high enough to put her feet over into the tube. She pushed down on his shoulders with her hands, raising herself high enough to get her hips centered over the tube and then she let go.

Sploosh! She was in the tube. "Oh, man! This water's cold."

Angel said, "You want me to get you out?"

"No. Pull me over to the middle of the pool. I want to see if I can move my legs."

Angel pulled on the tube, moving her to the upstream end of the pool. He held the tube steady there.

Neesie tried to move her legs. Her heart raced. She could move in the water! She kicked her legs slowly back and forth, feeling the resistance from the water, feeling the chill of the cold current. "Angel!" she gasped. "I can move my legs! I can move my legs! Thank God!"

Angel said, "In Jesus, amen."

Completely overcome with the joy of the moment,

Neesie held one hand around Angel's wrist. Tears rolled down her cheeks. She said, "I am going to walk again, Angel. After all these years, I am going to walk."

Angel said, "Angel help Neesie walk again."

When Neesie regained her composure, she said, "Okay, turn me loose and let's see if I can swim around."

Angel let go of the tube and Neesie started paddling with her hands and trying to kick her feet. She seemed to be going in every direction at once as the tube drifted down and bumped against the dam.

"Pull me back up there," she said.

He pulled her back to the upper end of the pool and turned her loose again. She was able to stay above the dam a little bit longer this time, but the current beat her again.

Angel was her tug boat. All afternoon, he pulled her upstream. She paddled and kicked as the current relentlessly carried her back down. Finally, she was too tired to try anymore. "It's no use," she said. "I can't keep myself away from the dam. Get me out."

Angel said, "Okay. Angel put you on the bank and then climb out and help you get into the wheelchair."

He lifted her up and set her on the bank. She held to the seat of the wheelchair and waited as he hopped out. After she was settled into her chair, Angel helped her dry off. She was frustrated. It seemed like the excitement of being able to move her legs was forgotten.

Angel knelt down in front of her and held her hands. "Neesie, it's a dance. Swimming is a dance. It's a water dance. You not fight water. Water not fight you. You see. Tomorrow you see. Tomorrow, when you in the water, you dance with the water, okay?"

Neesie looked at Angel, confused. "What?"

"Tomorrow, you not go straight up, straight down and fight water. Tomorrow, you go with water like dance. Water go all around. You go all around, too. Like water dance."

Angel left the tools at the picnic area. He needed to build some steps. He wanted Neesie to let herself down into the water. She needed to stop fighting the water and relax. Somehow, he understood that the density of the water was going to strengthen her legs. Neesie was going to walk.

Chapter Thirty Three

THAT NIGHT, NEESIE DREAMED SHE was in the pool alone. At first, there was total silence, then she began to hear the singing of the birds. She could hear the rush of the water as it cascaded over the dam. There was the wind in the trees, a soft whisper of a sound. The water seemed to pull her away gently, not in an aggressive way. She drifted along the dam and circled along the bank upstream, carried by an eddy in the current.

Far away, she thought she could hear a song, soft and soothing and full of promise. "Oh love of God, how rich and pure! How measureless and strong. It shall forevermore endure, the saints and angels' songs."

When she felt the dream fading as the morning sounds awakened her, she tried to hold on to her dream, but it was gone with the night. "It's a water dance," she whispered.

As soon as lunch was over that day, Neesie and Angel headed for their swimming pool. Angel dropped her into her tube and said, "Angel needs to make steps."

Neesie said, "Who does?"

Angel said, "Me. Angel. Okay, I do. You practice water dance while uh, I find some flat rocks."

Neesie said, "Wait, aren't you going to pull me upstream?"

"No, I make steps. You practice water dance."

Angel disappeared up the creek. He needed three big flat rocks to make the steps. He would have to dig into the bank to make an angled set of stairs from the creek to the ground.

Neesie looked around, thinking, "This is just like that dream, only the current isn't dancing me around the pool." She pulled herself along the dam, feeling for the undercurrent she had dreamed was there. She didn't feel the undercurrent, but she could feel the sandy bottom of the pool with her toes! Her mouth came open and she said, "Ahh," to herself. Her legs were barely strong enough to push her along. Near the bank, she found the undercurrent that ran against the flow of the creek. Now, moving was much easier, sort of like dancing on her tiptoes.

Angel returned with a large flat rock. He disappeared again and was soon back with two more. While he dug the slanted cut into the bank, Neesie told him about her dream, how peaceful it seemed, and how she thought she could hear a song.

"It went something like, 'Oh, love of God, how rich and pure'..." She stopped singing. "Did you ever hear a song like that?"

Angel said, "Yeah."

Neesie said, "Me neither. It sounded beautiful, though. Wait! You have heard it before?"

"Yeah."

"When?"

"Papa sang it to Angel one time when I was sick. I was still a baby, about three or four. Angel had the flu, maybe."

Neesie said, "He must have sung it when I was around and I don't remember it anymore."

Angel was digging with the mattock. "Sometimes, you dream memories. Sometimes, you dream hopes. You never, not never, dream when you're awake. When you're awake, you dance."

By the end of that day, there was a set of three steps. Angel walked down into the water. The last step was a little longer, but that didn't matter. He was going into the water anyway. He sat Neesie on the second step and pulled the tube up over her head and threw it on the bank. She was facing the water with her feet on the bottom step. The water came up to her knees. Angel stood in front of her and said, "See if you can lift yourself up to the top step. Angel Help Neesie."

Neesie said, "Let me try it by myself." She reached back and placed both of her hands on the top step and lifted her own body up. It was a hard thing to do, but she made it. Then, she lifted herself up on to the top of the bank. "I made it!"

Angel said, "Yeah, Neesie is strong."

The pool and steps were complete. Angel carried the tools over one shoulder while pushing Neesie's chair along with his free hand. Neesie talked about how they were going to swim some every day all summer long. She said that her legs would be strong soon, that she was going to walk and after she walked, she was going to run.

Angel asked, "Neesie, you forget something?"

Neesie looked back over her shoulder and asked, "I did? What?"

Angel said, "You silly sometimes. Neesie will dance, too."

Neesie gave a quiet answer. "Oh, yes. I'll dance, too." She raised her head and stared at the evening sky. Her eyes lost focus as she watched her imaginary self dancing and whirling to an orchestra of beautiful music.

Every sunny day that Summer, Neesie and Angel were in their swimming pool for at least a little while. Neesie's legs grew stronger. She gained twenty pounds and all of it was in her legs. Angel grew taller as well, His lean body was rippled with natural muscle. He was over six feet tall.

Both of them were deeply tanned from their heads to their toes.

During the third week of August, Angel told Neesie that it was time to tear down the dam. "Don't worry," he said, "Angel will throw the big rocks on the bank and pile them up. We build the pool back next Summer."

Neesie said, "Well, okay, if we have to, but I want you to do one more thing before you break it."

Angel said, "Okay."

As the sun was setting, Neesie told Angel to help her pull the tube over her head.

Angel said, "Okay, let me sit you on the step."

Neesie said, "No, Angel. Just pull the tube off and drop it in the water. I want to dance around in the pool with you, just us."

Angel pulled the tube up and dropped it. Neesie wrapped her arms around Angel's neck and said, "Put your arms around my waste and hold me up while we dance."

Angel said, "What we do for music?"

Neesie began to sing, "Soft as the voice of an angel, breathing a lesson unheard..."

Angel waltzed Neesie all around the pool while she sang. Even after she had stopped singing, she laid her head on his shoulder while he danced around the pool for a few more minutes.

She said, "I don't know what I would have done without you, Angel. I know God sent you to me."

Angel said, "Angel always help Neesie. Angel help Neesie walk in Jesus, amen."

Neesie said, "Amen."

The next morning before Neesie came to Angel's house, Angel took the shovel and broke down the dam, tossing all of the large rocks up on the bank. There was a slight pool where Angel had scooped the bottom up when he built the dam. Other than that, Easy Creek flowed lazily along as it had before.

He piled the rocks against the big shade tree and sat watching the water. He didn't quite understand how time passed so quickly, but he knew that he had become a young man, and Neesie was now a young lady. He also knew that he was made differently than everyone else. His time with Neesie would soon be over. He could remember everything about her, from the first time he pushed her wheelchair away from Mr. Green's store until yesterday when he danced with her in their handmade swimming pool.

"Angel help Neesie walk in Jesus, amen," he whispered to himself.

Chapter Thirty Four

IT WAS ON THE SAME day that Angel broke the dam that a car with Texas license plates pulled up to Green's store. A big man with coal black hair got out carrying a guitar. He walked through the door and spoke to Boots who was behind the counter.

"Good morning! Are you Mister Green?"

"No, sir. Mister Green retired a couple of years ago. I liked the name of the store so I didn't change it." He stuck his hand out. "Boots Daws, current proprietor."

The big man shook hands with Boots, "Melvin Johnson, world traveler, going nowhere in particular."

He had a manner about him. He was like a best friend who had been away, and he was on his way home, but he wanted to stop by to spend a few minutes with you first. Boots liked him immediately. "What can I do for you this morning, Mister Johnson?"

"Well, I have run a little short on cash and I don't steal. I can't say I want to pawn anything because you and I both know that I am never coming back this way, so I am going to try to talk you into buying my guitar."

Mr. Johnson held the guitar out and smiled. Boots laughed. "That has to be the best sales pitch I have ever heard." He took the guitar and looked at it.

"It says here that it's a Martin. Is that a good brand?"

"Only the best. That one there, new, would run you a thousand dollars."

Boots whistled. "I don't have that much money on hand, and it would be hard to resell something that expensive around here."

Mr. Johnson said, "That's the price of a new one. This one is vintage, probably used to belong to a famous singer. You see, I repair them and give them a new life. Guitars take a beating, especially the high dollar ones."

"Okay then, how much do you want for this one?"

Mr. Johnson narrowed his eyes. "How about a fill up on gas, a loaf of bread, a small jar of mayonnaise, a pack of bologna and a hundred dollars?"

Boots thought for a minute, and then called, "Bomains!"

Bomains came in from just outside of the back door. "Yes sir?"

"Look at this guitar and tell me if it's worth a hundred and fifty dollars."

Bomains took the guitar and strummed it clumsily.

Mr. Johnson said, "Let me show you, Bomains." He took the guitar and strummed a couple of chords, and then he finger picked a quick run of notes. He immediately changed into a professional. He began a performance, not at all discouraged by the fact that the entire audience was a country store keeper and his helper.

"Bomains?" he said, raising an eyebrow. He strummed his guitar. "Let me see your hands."

Bomains held his hands up and Mr. Johnson smiled, "Those hands ain't big are they?"

Bomains laughed and said, "No, sir, they're not."

Mr. Johnson strummed a couple more chords and said, "Something tells me you know this song."

"Twas in the merry month of May, when all the buds were swellin

Sweet William on his deathbed lay, for the love of Barbry Allen."

Mr. Johnson's voice was smooth, probably trained, but naturally beautiful as well.

When he started the second verse, Bomains joined in, singing in harmony.

"He sent his servant to the town, to the place where she was dwellin'

Saying you must come to my master dear, if your name be Barbry Allen.

Slowly, slowly she got up, and slowly she drew nigh him

And the only words that she did say, young man, I think you're dying."

Mr. Johnson said, "Boy, you can sing!"

Bomains smiled and said, "Let's finish the song."

So they continued.

"He turned his face unto the wall, for death was in him wellin'

Goodbye, Goodbye, to my friends all, be good to Barbry Allen.

When he was dead and laid in grave, she heard the death bells knellin

And every stroke to her did say, hardhearted Barbry Allen.

Oh Mother, Mother, dig my grave, make it both long and narrow

Sweet William died for true, true love, and I shall die for sorrow.

Oh Father, Father dig my grave, make it both long and narrow

Sweet William died on yesterday and I shall die tomorrow.

They buried her in the old churchyard, Sweet William there beside her

Out of William's heart there grew a rose, out of Barbry Allen's a brier

They grew and grew in the old church yard, till they could grow no higher

At the end they formed a true lover's bond, and the rose grew round the brier."

Boots stared at the two men, his heart touched. He turned away and muttered, "I guess I don't know anything about anybody around here."

Bomains said, "Boots, I think this guitar is worth a hundred and fifty dollars. I think I want to buy it."

Boots said, "Do you know how to play it?"

"Haven't got a clue, but if I can make it sound like he does, I should be famous before long."

Mr. Johnson said, "Boy, I believe you. What's your real name?"

"Bomains Grammercy."

Mr Johnson said, "No, it's...," but when he saw Bomains' face blush, he stopped talking.

A look passed between them and Mr. Johnson said, "Here's our deal: a hundred dollars cash, a tank of gas, and some groceries. Y'all get the guitar and I'll get back on the road."

Bomains pulled out his wallet and counted eight twenties. He handed them to Boots. Boots gave Mr. Johnson five of the twenties, and told him to get what he wanted while Bomains pumped his gas.

When Mr. Johnson came out with his bag of food, he called Bomains over to the front door of his car. He had a pen and a notepad in his hands. "Son, give me your address and phone number. I know a few agents who might want to talk to you."

Bomains said, "Uh, I'm only seventeen. I can't sign any legal documents."

Mr. Johnson said, "Young man, you'll be twenty one before you know it."

Bomains' whole body tensed. "I am not going to give you any information about me. Besides, like you said, you'll never come down this road again."

Mr. Johnson said, "I'm sorry, Bomains. I'm trying to do you a favor."

Bomains said, "You think you know something, and I appreciate the offer, but I don't want to talk about the future right now."

Mr. Johnson apologized again, then left.

When Bomains came back into the store, Boots said, "He seemed like a nice fellow."

Bomains said, "Yeah. He's selling Martin guitars for a hundred dollars."

Bomains picked the guitar up and ran his fingers along the neck, picking notes like a master player.

Boots said, "Hey! I thought you said you couldn't play one."

Bomains propped the guitar against the wall and said, "Everybody has a hobby, Boots."

Boots looked at the door, looked at Bomains, totally confused. "Who was that guy, Bomains?"

Bomains said, "I don't know, but he's not coming back." He went out the back door of the store, back to the work he had been doing.

Chapter Thirty Five

SEPTEMBER BROUGHT THEIR JUNIOR YEAR of school.
Bomains returned to his seat at the lunch table. Something
had changed about him. He was naturally quiet, but his
mood was different. He seemed to be jumpy, distracted
and nervous. He was constantly watching the doors as if
expecting somebody to come into the lunch room. There
was obviously somebody that he didn't want to see.

Neesie was a beautiful young woman now. At seventeen, she was physically grown. Drawn to her natural
friendliness and beautiful smile, more of the girls stopped
by their table at lunch to chat. Finally, she was making
new friends.

Angel was content to sit quietly while Neesie talked
with her friends. Bomains only talked a little, usually
about one of their classes or about the store, so Angel
ate his lunch in silence, only speaking when asked a

question. His answers were usually one or two words. Other than at home or at Neesie's house, he didn't have much to say.

There was one particular person who had noticed Neesie. Even though most of his time was taken up by football, Ace Kyker couldn't change how he felt about her. Every time he saw Neesie, his heart would begin to race. He was desperate to talk to her. There were several girls in his class who were interested in him, but he was only interested in Neesie.

One day, he came over to the lunch table where she sat with Bomains and Angel. When Bomains saw him approaching, he stood up.

Ace put his hand out and said, "It's okay. I just want to talk to Neesie for a second."

Bomains clenched his fists and said, "That's probably not a good idea, Ace."

Ace's shoulders slumped. "Look, I'm trying to apologize for what I did. You can't deny me the opportunity to make things right."

"Yes I can." Bomains had spoken softly, but the message was unmistakable.

Neesie said, "Say what you want to, Ace."

Bomains stepped in front of Ace. "You have nothing to say."

With a quiet, but intense tone, Angel said, "Bomains, you not!"

Seeing the possibility for another scene that he couldn't afford, Ace reached around Bomains and handed

Neesie a folded note. "Here," he said. When she took the note, he turned around and left.

Neesie closed her hand over the note and didn't say a word. As soon as Ace was gone, she started talking as if the event had never happened. Bomains sat in his chair until it was time to go to the next class. He appeared to be in a very bad mood. As he stood up to leave the lunch table, Angel grabbed his arm. "Bomains, what happened last year, that fight, you got mad. I got mad. Everybody mad. That's not wrong, but you not hate Ace. If you hate, that's wrong."

Bomains said, "Angel, you don't understand. You can't be friends with somebody like Ace."

Angel said, "Angel knows that. Sometimes, I don't say things right, but this time maybe. Neesie not friends with Ace. Angel not friends with Ace, but Bomains can be friends with Ace. Ace make Bomains a good friend, probably."

Bomains started to argue, and then he remembered the few times before when Angel had told him something and he had not listened. He said, "I'll think about what you're saying, Angel. You're right, I shouldn't hate Ace."

As Angel was pushing Neesie out of the lunch room, she opened the note, read it, and tossed it into the trash can as they went out through the door.

That afternoon when Angel was giving Neesie her massage, she asked Angel, "Don't you want to know what Ace's note said?"

Angel said, "Yeah."

"It said that Ace was sorry that he had hurt someone so beautiful. He wanted to try to make it up to me by having me over to his house for supper one night. He wants to show me and his parents that he is truly sorry."

Angel asked, "You go see Ace?"

"Nope."

"You believe he's sorry?"

"I guess so, but you were right when you were talking to Bomains. I think Ace is kind of mean right now. Bomains would be a good influence for him, but you and I don't need to be around him. He doesn't know how to treat people like us."

Angel said, "What we like?"

Neesie was trying to think of the right words to answer Angel when she noticed that he was looking at her with that half smile of his. She gasped. "You big..."

"Dummy?"

"No! Angel, you're not funny!"

"Then why Neesie laughing?"

Neesie half yelled, "I'm not laughing!" And then she started laughing.

Angel didn't laugh. Inside, he probably did. He was his father's son.

There was a new exercise they were doing since the swimming pool was gone. Angel would stand Neesie on her feet in front of him and support her weight by putting his hands under her arms and holding her. Then, she would try to squat down and stand back up. The progress was slow, but both Neesie and Angel could feel the strength continue to grow in her legs. Sometimes, she would growl as she pushed, trying to use every bit of the strength she already had. This could cause her back muscles to spasm. Angel would rub her lower back with olive oil and place a heating pad over her back and hips.

No secret can be kept forever and their secret about her legs was not going to last much longer. It was the olive oil that gave them away.

Chapter Thirty Six

IT IS DURING THE FINAL two years of high school that the parents and the teachers become most apprehensive about their children. Their bodies are changing. Everything they can imagine, whatever someone suggests, they are likely to try. Their world is a field of booby traps, but the young believe it is a playground.

Laura Dell and Rachel were not any different than other parents. They were well aware of the tragedies that can alter the lives of teenagers or snuff them out suddenly. With Bomains working at the store during the afternoons, he was almost considered a family member, and both Laura Dell and Rachel thought of Neesie and Angel as a son and a daughter.

When Neesie asked for tight exercise pants for Christmas and some small six and eight pound lifting weights, Rachel bought them. She wondered if a certain boy at school had caught Neesie's eye. There was no stopping the clock, no turning back the seasons, and Rachel could still remember the sting of losing her first love. She prayed that Neesie would meet a boy who fully understood her situation.

The new year turned and there was no boy, no phone calls, no visitors. Rachel noticed how Neesie and Angel were often leaning their faces so very close to each other and talking in hushed whispers. She could also see a new glow on Neesie's face as if she had been promised something, and its delivery was expected soon. Adding the fact that Neesie was more full bodied than she had been a few months ago, Rachel became suspicious.

Looking back over the last few years, she realized how everyone had been so busy with the store and other activities that they had left Neesie and Angel to take care of each other without much adult supervision. They had all assumed that the innocence of their children would automatically renew itself. Now, she feared the worst.

She was always noticing the light stains on the sheets from the massage bed when she would wash them. For years, she had assumed it was perspiration, nothing else. Now, she wondered what it was. This time, when she changed the sheets she smelled of the area where the stain was, but there was no smell of sweat or anything else. What was it? She dared not accuse them. She was almost afraid to ask Neesie about what all of the secret whispering and smiling that was going on was about, but there was no way of avoiding the dreaded moment of discovery. Her heart sank and she whispered a private prayer for her daughter and Angel.

Rachel picked Neesie and Angel up on a cold Friday afternoon at the school. As she was driving home, she said, "Kids, we have something to do this afternoon, so Neesie, you won't have time for your massage."

Neesie was immediately on guard. She said, "What do we have to do, Mommy? My massage won't take but a few minutes, and it really helps my back."

"We'll talk about it in a few minutes. We can drop Angel off at his house. I'll tell you when we get home."

Now, Angel was sitting straight up. He didn't say anything, but the tension in both Rachel's and Neesie's voices was hard to miss. He didn't know what Neesie had done, but he thought she must be in bad trouble.

Neesie, having done nothing outside of her daily routine, worried that something very bad had happened, and she didn't know what it could be. Beginning to panic, she asked, "Mommy, what's wrong?"

Rachel said, "Nothing's wrong, Sweetheart. There's just something we need to do right quick."

Neesie looked at Angel, a great worry in her eyes. Angel mouthed the word, "What?" Neesie raised her hands, palms up and shoulder high and shook her head. She didn't know.

When Angel got out of the car at his house, he was completely confused. He walked through the door, his mind in a fog. He wondered why Neesie was in trouble. It must be bad, he thought. He went into his private back room. There was nobody there but Shady and him. He turned on the Rocky music and began to jump rope. Shady hopped over the rope and jumped with him for a while. Then he hit the heavy bag and after he tired of that, he punched the speed bag. It was only an hour until his Papa came home, but to Angel it seemed like the longest hour of his life.

When Rachel helped Neesie roll through the door at their house, she said, "Go into the living room and wait for me. We need to have a long talk, young lady."

Again, Neesie asked, "Mommy, will you please tell me what's wrong?"

In a voice she had seldom used with her daughter, Rachel said, "I think you know what's wrong."

Neesie said, "I don't know, Mommy. I promise you I don't know." She rolled into the living room and waited.

Rachel took a minute to steady herself. Her daughter was the joy of her life. She would rather walk through fire than to face this moment. She walked into the living room and sat down. She took Neesie's hand in hers. Her heart hurt so bad as she began to talk.

"Neesie, I haven't been a very good mother. I should have spent more time with you than I did. I should have given you guidance. You are the best daughter in the world, and there is nothing that can make me stop loving you."

Neesie looked at her mother with her forehead bunched up in wrinkles and her mouth half open. She shook her head in a quick short movement. "What is she talking about," she wondered, but didn't say anything.

Rachel said, "Neesie, is there something you need to tell me?"

Neesie didn't respond. She stared at her mother, her face blank.

Rachel tried again. "Have you and Angel been doing something that you shouldn't be doing?"

Neesie gasped, "Mother! Have you lost your mind? Do you think Angel and I have...? How could you believe such a thing?"

Rachel said, "Now, Neesie, you are a very beautiful girl. I know things can happen all of a sudden and..."

Very firmly, Neesie said, "Mommy, nothing has happened."

"Well, then, I want you to explain why you wanted those tight fitting clothes for Christmas. And why are you lifting those little weights all of a sudden, and why do you have such a beautiful glow about you, and why are you and your "Angel" always holding hands and whispering all of the time?"

Angry because of the way Rachel had said Angel's name with distaste, Neesie screamed, "You don't know, do you, Mommy? You don't know!"

Before she could stop herself, Rachel screamed back, "Oh, I know! I can see the stains on the sheets from your exercise bed. I can see the loving words that pass between you two. And, you know what? For you to sit there and yell at me is as bad as anything you have already done. Don't sit there and tell me nothing's going on!"

Neesie screamed so loud that it hurt her throat, "Don't sit here? Don't sit here! Since when did you want me to not sit here? Mommy, you're wrong! You don't even know what's going on with Angel and me. When Daddy gets home, I'm going to fix you good!"

Rachel, still angry, but also hurting so bad that tears were pouring from her eyes, said, "Yes, when your Daddy gets home, you fix me, because I'm pretty sure he's going to want to talk to Angel and his family as soon as you get through fixing me!"

Neesie burst into tears. "Mommy, please don't make me have surgery. It will ruin everything. It will ruin my whole life." She wheeled herself away to her bedroom, sobbing.

Rachel sat in her chair, stunned. "Surgery," she whispered. She stood up and walked over and tapped on Neesie's bedroom door. "Neesie, why do you think I am going to make you have surgery?" She could hear her daughter sobbing behind the door, but she dared not go in.

"Because, Mommy, you believe more in the doctor than you do in God. You believe more in medicine than you do in miracles."

"What miracle, Neesie?"

Neesie screamed, "I want my Daddy!"

Chapter Thirty Seven

WHEN J. P. CAME THROUGH the door, Angel was standing just inside, waiting for him. J. P. immediately knew something was wrong. "Angel?"

Angel took a step towards his father. "Papa," he said and put his arms around J. P.'s shoulders.

J. P. grabbed Angel by the elbows and pushed him away a little so he could see his eyes. "What's the matter? Are you sick?"

"No, Papa. Neesie is in trouble."

A chill ran through J. P., physically shaking him. "What king of trouble?"

"Angel don't know, Papa. But maybe bad."

Angel looked very pale, like he might faint. J. P. lead him over to a chair at the dining table and sat him down. He said, "Now, what makes you think Neesie's in trouble?"

"Rachel told her no massage. They had to do something. Neesie don't know. Rachel brought me home and then she took Neesie home. Neesie's in trouble, Papa."

Angel began to shake and he crossed his arms, trying to hold back panic and tears and an overwhelming fear that he was not going to see his lifelong promise to Neesie come true. He said, "Papa, Angel helps Neesie. I always help Neesie. I help Neesie now."

J.P. wasn't sure what to do. He said, "Wait a minute, Son. Let me call Boots at the store and see what's going on. It may not be as big of a deal as you think." But even as he was dialing the telephone, a horrible dread was coming over him like a dark wave.

When Boots answered the phone, J. P. said, "Hey, I just came in from work and Angel is very upset. He thinks something's happening to Neesie. Boots, he's scared to death and so am I, now. What's going on?"

Boots said, "I don't know of anything that's going on. Let me call the house and I'll call you right back."

Boots hung up and J. P. stood beside Angel, rubbing his shoulders while he waited for the phone to ring. After about five minutes, Boots called back. He said, "J. P., I don't know what's happening. Rachel was crying, and she is so upset that I could hardly understand a word. I'm closing the store now. Laura Dell is going to ride with me to the house. I'll honk when we go by and I want you to bring Angel with you. It must be something bad, J. P. But I don't know what it is."

After just a few minutes, J. P. heard the car horn as Boots passed the house. Angel jumped when he heard it. J. P. said, "Come on, Angel. Let's go see if we can help Neesie."

When they came out of the door, Angel started running up the road. J. P. started to call him back, but he thought, no, let him run. To him it will feel like he's getting there faster.

J. P. pulled into the Daws' driveway and waited for Angel to finish the last fifty yards of his run. Angel stood with his hands on his thighs, gasping for breath. After a short wait, J. P. asked, "Are you ready to go in?"

Angel took one more deep breath and nodded that he was. J. P. knocked lightly on the door and stepped inside with Angel close behind him. Rachel was sitting on a couch in their living room, wiping her eyes with a tissue. Laura Dell was sitting beside her with her arms around her shoulders.

J. P. gave Laura Dell a questioning look. Laura Dell shook her head slightly. "Where's Boots?", J. P. asked.

Laura Dell said, "He's in there talking to Neesie, trying to find out what's going on." She came over to J. P. and whispered, "They've had a terrible fight, J. P."

"What about?"

Laura Dell pulled J. P. away so Angel couldn't hear. "I'm not sure. Rachel is so torn up that I can't figure it out. At first it seemed like she thought Neesie is... you know. But now, she thinks maybe something's wrong with her back. Something Neesie and Angel have been keeping from us."

J. P. said, "I wonder why she thinks Neesie is, uh that way. Did she catch them doing something?"

"No, but she said there have been stains on the sheets a lot lately."

J. P. called Angel over. Under his breath, he said, "Son, what's causing the stains on Neesie's massage bed sheets?"

Angel said, "Papa, sometimes when Angel puts olive oil on hands, it runs down on the sheets."

"Olive oil?"

"Yes, Papa. Momma gives me olive oil. Angel anoints Neesie's back and helps Neesie's back in Jesus. Amen."

Laura Dell said, "Ohhhh! That explains it."

J. P. said, "I'll be back in a few minutes. Boots needs to know about the olive oil if Neesie hasn't told him." He went to the bedroom door and tapped. The door opened and he stepped through.

Laura Dell sat down with Rachel again. She whispered the explanation about the stains, about Angel anointing Neesie's back with olive oil and praying for her. Angel stood still. His face showed no emotion.

Rachel laid her head against Laura Dell's shoulder and began to cry again. "What have I done?" she sobbed. "Oh my daughter, my friends, and our poor Angel. I'm so sorry. I'm so sorry."

Laura Dell said, "Hush, Rachel. It's okay. It's going to be okay."

The bedroom door opened and Neesie came rolling out, followed by Boots and J. P. who had their heads bowed. Their eyes were red from wiped away tears. Neesie went over to Angel and spun her chair around to face the four parents.

Boots sat down next to Rachel and J.P. took a chair near the couch. Boots said, "Let's hear it, kids. What the heck is going on?"

Neesie's voice failed her the first time she tried to speak. "I'm still... I'm still a... maiden. Mommy, you didn't know about the olive oil. I guess I should have explained about that."

Rachel said, "It's okay, Baby."

Angel said, "A place on her back, a knot, hard, and it hurt Neesie. Angel anoint like preacher at church and pray in Jesus. The knot got soft and smaller. It's gone now."

Rachel and Boots looked at each other, shocked.

Neesie said, "After the knot disappeared, I could feel my legs. When it snowed, and Angel and I played in the snow, we had to come in because my legs were cold. I could feel them."

All four of the parents gasped. Rachel said, "Neesie! Why didn't you tell us? We could have called the doctor."

Neesie started to explain why they didn't tell anyone, but the more she explained, the more her emotions came out and took over her voice and her words.

"My legs were beginning to move. I could feel them when Angel did my massage. At first, they just tingled, then I could really feel them. The anointing oil was what did it. Plus the prayers." She looked at her mother's face and said, "I didn't tell you because I was afraid you would call the doctor. I was afraid he would want to do surgery."

She beat her fist on the arm rest of the wheelchair. "I'm not going to have surgery! I don't need surgery! I need a miracle!"

She glared at her mother. "I've heard you talking to the doctor! I've heard you talking to Daddy! You don't believe I'll ever walk! Well, you should have seen me in that pool in Easy Creek. I was kicking around in my floating tube all by myself."

Angel said, "Water dance."

Neesie said, "Yeah, the water dance. Angel taught me how to dance in the water. That's why my body is bigger. That's why my face is glowing, because I'm going to have a miracle. I'm going to walk! I'm going to dance! I'm going to run like the police are chasing me!"

Neesie started waving her arms as her voice grew louder and stronger. "I dreamed of the water dance and I did it! I have dreamed that I will get up out of this ugly, clumsy, stinking wheelchair and dance with Angel, and I am going to do it! I hate this chair! I am not willing to accept staying in this chair! I am going to see this chair in the garbage can before long. God is going to get me out of this chair because a doctor can't!"

Breathing heavily, she grabbed a hold of Angel's hand. "A doctor can't repair my back, but an angel can. I will give you my wheelchair, but I will die before I let you take my angel. Angel believes that God is going to help me walk again and I believe Angel."

Angel said, "Angel help Neesie walk in Jesus. Amen"

Neesie said, "Stand in front of me, Angel. Be ready to catch me."

Angel stepped in front of the wheelchair. Rachel started to say something, but Boots squeezed her hand.

Angel's tall body almost hid Neesie completely, but there was nothing to muffle Neesie's determined growl of effort. She said, "I got it, Angel." And Angel stepped aside to reveal Neesie standing, her legs trembling. After about five seconds, Angel caught her and steadied her as she fell slowly back into the wheelchair.

Rachel said, "Oh, my sweet Jesus. Oh, my sweet babies."

J. P. jumped out of his chair and shouted, "Glory!" He raised both hands into the air and laughed. "Glory to the most high God!" His voice was full and deep. His soul was proclaiming a miracle.

Boots stared at Angel. "You are an Angel, aren't you?"

Angel said, "Yeah, in Jesus. Amen."

Neesie smiled and said, "Y'all, that was the first time."

After a few more minutes, Neesie said, "You can't tell anybody. You have to all keep the secret like we have. I'm not going to wobble around with a set of crutches and risk a bad fall. I'm going to stand up one day and walk away from this chair forever. And, Mommy, you can't tell the doctor because he's not the healer. God is."

Rachel said, "Don't worry, Sweetie, I won't."

Chapter Thirty Eight

ALTHOUGH THE NEXT MORNING WAS cold, there was a warm feeling in the Daws house. Boots hurried off to work, almost floating as he grabbed his cup of coffee. Rachel helped Neesie get dressed, and they sat at the breakfast table talking about anything except the night before. Rachel held Neesie's hand and kissed it.

Neesie said, "I need a massage. My back is stiff and I need to do my leg exercises."

Rachel said, "If Angel isn't here by nine, we'll give him a call."

At the Higgins house, J. P. decided to go and help at the store so Laura Dell could be at home. That way she could be available if there was any lingering drama. The shock and joy of what Neesie and Angel were doing for the last year without anyone finding out still seemed hard to believe. They were all going to have to pay closer attention to their children. Laura Dell decided that spying on them at least a little bit was acceptable.

As soon as Angel ate his breakfast, he grabbed his coat and said, "Angel go see Neesie." He was gone without waiting for an answer. Laura Dell looked out of the window and watched him go. He was walking at a quick pace. She lost sight of him within a few long strides. It occurred to her that they had all seen Angel through a window, through a lens in their minds that focused on the few things that he could not quite do. She thought of the Bible verse that said, "through the glass darkly." She whispered to herself, "It does not appear what we shall become, but when He appears, we shall be like Him."

It was a slow day at the store. Bomains was able to handle most of the work which gave Boots and J. P. a chance to have a private conversation.

In his office with the door closed, Boots said, "Friend, was it hard for you to fall asleep last night?"

"Not really. As soon as I got some food in me and a shower and and my heart slowed down from two hundred beats a minute and I prayed for about an hour, I fell right off to sleep."

Boots shook his head. "I realized something about myself. I kept a better eye on my boys in the army than I ever kept on my own daughter, and she's in a wheelchair. I have to be a better father than that, and a better man."

J. P. said, "What dawned on me last night at about midnight is the fact that we think something's a little bit off with Angel because he's autistic, but he solves complex problems. I thought he was making that little pool in the creek because, in his simple way of thinking, it was a place to have fun. But from the beginning, he was building an exercise pool for Neesie's legs. He's different, but he's not simple minded."

Boots slapped his desk and said, "Hey, there's something we need to start looking at. Angel has talent. He's an organizer. He's a planner. He gets things done. There's a future for him."

"Do you want to let him start working on Saturday mornings here?" J. P. asked. "Can we see what he actually can do?"

Boots agreed. "Let's start while business is slow and see how he does. Maybe we will find a set of tasks that he excels at."

When Boots approached Bomains with the idea of having Angel at the store on Saturdays, he thought it was a good idea. Bomains said, "He needs to go into public life a little bit more, plus we can always use another set of strong arms around here."

So, a new part of Angel's life began. He worked on Saturdays from seven in the morning until noon. If Bomains took a Saturday off, Angel would work until three in the afternoon. There was an immediate effect on the appearance of the store.

Angel was an organizer. Soon, he not only knew where every product was located, he knew where it logically should be. During the early morning, between seven and nine, Angel and Bomains relocated products according to their use. They located everything according to the likelihood and frequency of its sale. When customers walked in, they were likely to see just what they were looking for or find it easily. Some days, Angel seemed to watch the clock, and he was out the door as soon as it was noon. Other times, he would be so involved in his work that he may work over an hour. Stillness was not in his nature. He relaxed by doing.

During the month of March, as Spring approached, Bomains seemed to grow moody. He didn't gripe or slack in his work, but there was a sadness beginning to grow in his appearance. Boots could watch him for a minute and sense that he was struggling. Well, he wasn't going let something else surprise him.

One afternoon, as they were closing up for the day, Boots said, "Bomains, I want you to hang around for a minute if you're not in a hurry."

Bomains said, "Sure."

They walked into the office and Boots said, "Sit down and let's talk about something. I need your input."

Bomains sat in a chair facing the desk and Boots started asking questions. He said, "I have noticed for the last few weeks that something is bothering you. You know I'm your friend. I want the absolute best for you, so if something is going on and I can help, please let me know."

Bomains took a deep, deep breath and let it out. He said, "Boots, do you remember a country singer named Billy Granite?"

Boots thought a second and said, "Yeah, a long time ago, he sang a real sad song, One Way Street to the Graveyard, or something like that."

Bomains said, "That was my grandfather."

"Oh, didn't he die pretty young?

"Yes sir, he was thirty four when he died."

Boots had a feeling he was about to hear a bad story. He cleared his throat. "How did he die, son?"

"His career killed him. Pills, alcohol, two hundred and fifty shows a year, women sneaking on his bus, smoke from cigarettes, it all killed him. In a ten year run, he wore out his heart and liver."

Something clicked in Boots' memory. "Wait a minute. I read something about him. He always saved, like a fourth of his show earnings and all of his royalties in a hidden account. He left a pretty good fortune to his son."

Bomains said, "Yes, he did. His son is my dad."

Boots was wondering how the death of a grandfather he never knew could cause bad feelings for Bomains.

Bomains said, "His son is Gary Grammer."

Boots' eyes turned cloudy. "Oh, Bomains."

Bomains said, "I was five years old when it happened. Dad took my grandfather's guitar and vowed that he would spread the Gospel with songs. I don't know how many songs he wrote, and he wasn't a fake, either. He loved people. He didn't want anyone to wind up like his daddy. Momma said he was gone a lot, but she never had any reason to think Dad was doing anything but singing Gospel music."

Bomains had a hard time telling the story of what happened to his father. "They were building a big new church in Texas, and they decided to have one last singing in their old church. Dad said it was very old with hardwood floors and it had the best acoustics of any building he ever sang in."

Boots said, "I remember the news reporter saying it was old."

Bomains continued the tale of what happened. "He was singing one of his powerful songs about the love of God, and the church was packed full because all of the big groups were there that night. Anyway, the people got to jumping around and stomping their feet and all of a sudden, the floor and the stage fell sixteen feet into the basement."

Boots was picturing the episode in his mind, hundreds of worshipers disappearing in a cloud of dust like the earth had swallowed them.

Bomains said, "Big pieces of the sound equipment fell on my dad. He was broken all to pieces. His arms, his hands, his ribs, there wasn't much left of him. He never did recover. He's only forty five years old and he hobbles around like he's eighty. His voice is bad, and sometimes it's hard to understand what he's saying. The only thing that's not broken about him is his spirit. Momma loves him just as much as she ever did. She takes good care of him."

Boots could see how the situation might wear on a boy's spirit. He said, "Yeah, that's got to be tough on her."

Bomains squirmed in his chair and said, "Boots, that's not what's eating me alive. As long as I can remember, Dad's been like he is. Momma has been taking care of him. They accept that sometimes tragedy comes and it's really bad."

Boots didn't want to ask the next question, but he was the one who called this meeting, so he said, "What's bothering you, Bomains?"

"It's the guitar. The more I play it, the more I want to sing. The more I want to sing, the more I worry about what will happen to me. My grandfather is dead, dead early. My dad is broken all to pieces. But I can't get away from music. It's like being in love with a box full of broken glass. If I completely embrace it, I'm going to wind up bleeding in a hundred places. If I sit and stare at it long enough, I'm going to jump in. There is nothing in me that wants to turn my back and walk away. I want to sing, Boots. I want to."

Boots didn't know how he should answer Bomains. The young man had talent. His voice was one of those that touches a person's heart. When he sang, he sang the human struggle. He finally asked, "Why don't you start small and see if a local stage will help you scratch the itch?"

Bomains said, "I am thinking about being in the school talent show in May. Who knows? I might get stage fright."

Boots laughed. He stood up and they walked out of the store. "You're not afraid of a stage, son, and you know it."

Under his breath, Bomains said, "Yeah, that's what scares me."

Chapter Thirty Nine

IN MID-APRIL, AS THE SCHOOL year was winding down, the principal posted the list of acts who would be performing. Many of the students were disappointed when Angel's name didn't appear. When several students asked him why he wasn't performing, he said, "Bomains will sing. Angel will listen in the audience."

One morning, as Bomains was changing classes, he happened to pass Ace Kyker in the hallway. Ace, expecting no response, nodded and said, "Hey, Bomains."

Bomains surprised Ace by answering, "Hey, Ace, how's it going?"

Ace stopped to talk for a minute, "Okay, I guess you heard I got a scholarship. It's a small college, so you won't be seeing me on television."

Bomains smiled and said, "At least it's a full scholarship, right? What are you going to major in?"

"Marketing. I hope to work my way into event promotions. That way I will get to be around the bright lights even if I'm not the one the crowd is cheering for."

Both of the boys laughed, a quick chuckle. Ace said, "Hey, speaking of bright lights, I saw your name on the talent show roster. What are you going to do?"

"I'm going to play my guitar and sing a song, I guess."

Ace said, "I didn't know you could play a guitar. What kind of music do you play?"

Bomains quietly answered, "Ballads mostly, you know, old folk songs. I don't do much rock and roll yet. I'm not quite ready for that."

Ace slapped him on the shoulder and said, "Well, you have to start somewhere, right? I'll tell you this, you have the face of a singer, all those sad eyes and everything. I'm sure you'll be great."

Bomains said, "Thanks."

Ace turned to go, and then turned back. "Bomains," he said, "if there's anything I can do to help you, just ask. I owe you a lot. You changed my life."

Bomains said, "Me?" before he could stop the word from coming out.

Ace smiled a humble smile and said, "Yeah! A fellow gets to do a lot of self evaluation when he's being choked to death. It's easy to see who you are right before the lights go out."

Ace waved and headed down the hall to his next class. Bomains watched him go and said, "Hmph." Then he was on his way as well.

The month of May came, all blossoms and sunshine. The store was stocked, the fields were plowed and the seeds were planted. The Easy Creek Farm didn't get any larger that year. Laura Dell and Rachel hoped to have a more productive crop than the year before. Angel kept a running tally of which seeds were selling the most and which were not selling too well. It looked like folks were skittish about planting cucumbers, cantaloupes, and watermelons. The bad yield last year had affected them the most, so Laura Dell and Rachel decided that they would take a big gamble and plant what the other small farmers didn't plant. They planted only a few tomatoes, expecting a surplus of them.

Rachel measured the distance between the little hills and mixed the fertilizer with manure and some other compost. Everything was going to grow on a vine this year except a few rows of okra.

The night of the talent show came, and Neesie made her demand again. Bomains must be the last act. The principal laughed and said, "Young lady, this is turning into a tradition with you, I think."

Neesie said, "I'll be graduating next year, so this time and one more is all I will ask. It's not that big of a deal." She wheeled herself away, knowing she would have her request honored.

Last year, Angel had stolen the show with his juggling act. This year, the performers were serious about improving their craft. Every act was better. Whether they were singing, dancing, or performing skits and stunts, the show was a display of impressive talent.

Bomains was a little bit worried that the audience would be tired of cheering and clapping by the time he had his turn. Finally, his name was announced.

"Ladies and gentlemen, for the first time on stage in his life, Bomains Grammercy." A single light lit the stage. Bomains stood in front of the microphone with his hands motionless on the guitar. He paused for a long count. In his mind, he thought, "one... two... three... four." His left hand moved along the neck of the guitar, forming the chords as his fingers picked the notes, a beautiful soft tune. When the audience was beginning to think that it was an instrumental performance, Bomains let the world hear that beautiful tenor voice for the very first time.

"Starry, starry night. Paint your palette blue and gray. Look out on a summer's day with eyes that know the darkness in my soul...."

The audience sat, silent, encircled by a voice they didn't know, a soul who they should have recognized but didn't.

"Now I understand, what you tried to say to me, how you suffered for your sanity, and how you tried to set them free.

They would not listen, they did not know how...."

Oh, the voice was too pure, the emotion was so raw. Bomains' face reflected every word of the ballad. His guitar seemed to sing along with his voice.

Neesie felt like she was trapped in the song. She wanted to put her hands over her ears, but her heart held desperately to every word.

"For they could not love you, but still your love was true, and when no hope was left in sight on that starry, starry night, you took your life as lovers often do,

But I could have told you Vincent, this world was never meant for one as beautiful as you...

Finally, but way too soon, it was done.

"They would not listen, they're not listening still. Perhaps they never will...."

He stopped. Dead still, head down. Total silence.

One... two... three... four...

Bomains raised his head and looked out to the audience, smiled and waved his hand and said, "Thank you!"

The crowd erupted in applause! The roar continued for a good three minutes. Bomains assumed the role of M. C. and shouted into the microphone, "Let's get all of the performers out here! Come on out, y'all! How about a big hand! What a great show!"

The performers came out and lined up along the stage, taking a couple of bows. The audience left happy. Some of the girls were still wiping their eyes as they walked slowly out of the auditorium. "Who could have known?", one girl asked her friend. "He's so quiet at school. I never thought, ahh, he sounded so beautiful, so sad."

Boots sat in his seat, even as the crowd was going away. He held Rachel's hand tightly, but never said a word. If he needed to wipe something off of his cheek, he didn't.

Chapter Forty

THAT SUMMER, BOMAINS BEGAN TO bring his guitar to the store. He would play and sing while he and Boots ate their lunch. One day, Boots said, "Bomains, where do you go to church?"

"I don't go anywhere. I read my Bible at night. I pray, usually when something bad has happened, or when I'm unsure of what to do about something."

"Well, listen, our church homecoming is the last Sunday in June. I believe everybody in the church would love it if Neesie and you got up and sang at least one song. We have a group coming to sing, but y'all can sing while they're taking a break."

Bomains looked doubtful. "Boots, are you sure? I've sung for Neesie, and I've heard her sing, but we have never sung a song together."

Boots said, "I am sure she would love it. Let me talk to her tonight. You two can pick out a song and practice."

"Okay, Boots. You're the boss. If she wants to do it, I'm in."

That afternoon, Boots found Neesie and Angel at the picnic area. Angel was knee deep in Easy Creek, setting the big rocks in place to build the dam back. Neesie was standing on the bank, her wheelchair a couple of steps away. She was talking as usual, giving instructions on how to set the rocks in a straight line. Angel appeared to be ignoring her as he set them in a slight arc across the creek, like they should be.

Boots smiled and said, "Daughter, how long have you been standing there?"

"About an hour."

"What!"

Neesie laughed, "Okay, maybe five minutes, but I really can make it to ten minutes before my legs start shaking and I have to sit down."

Boots hugged her and kissed her on the forehead. He said, "If you tell me you can stand there until the sun comes up tomorrow, I'll believe you. There is nothing that you can't do."

Neesie looked up at her daddy and smiled. "You still can't tell anybody. I am not going to take a chance of tripping and falling until I am sure my back can handle it. As far as anyone is concerned, the only way I travel is with the wheelchair."

Boots said, "Got it. By the way, how would you like to sing a duet with Bomains at homecoming? Get with him and pick out a song and practice. When the group that's going to sing takes a break, y'all take the stage."

Suddenly, Neesie was looking at something far away; the future, the church, the song, Bomains. She said, "Tell Bomains I want to do it if he does."

"He does, because I asked him about it today," Boots said. "Now all that's left is for you to pick out a song."

"I have it picked out already," Neesie answered.

Angel stood up from placing a rock and said, "The Love of God," and reached up on the bank to grab another boulder.

Neesie said, "Angel!"

Angel looked at Boots with that half-smile on his face.

Boots patted Neesie on the head and laughed. "You can call Bomains when you get through with building the pool. He'll be thrilled." He started back to the Higgins' house, leaving the dam building to the younger generation.

Neesie said, "Angel, how did you know?"

Angel tried to answer, but the correct words seemed to elude him. "You dreamed a song. Somebody says, at a special time, you supposed to sing. Neesie, you sing the dream song. Always, every time, you do that. You know that."

Neesie said, "Yeah, that makes sense."

The next day, Boots told Bomains what song Neesie wanted to sing. Bomains said, "That's a powerful song when the Spirit is moving. I hope we can handle it."

Boots nodded. "I'm not worried."

Bomains remembered something. "I told Momma I was probably going to sing. She wants to bring Dad if he feels up to it. That's alright, isn't it?"

"Son, it's more than alright. It's an honor."

The next Sunday, Bomains came to church and sat with Angel and Neesie. After church, they all ate lunch at Angel's house and went into the dancing room to practice. Bomains became the second person to accept an invitation into the dancing room.

He looked around, unimpressed with the simple furnishings. There was an open closet with Angel's few flashy outfits, a tape and CD player, the boxing equipment, and a couple of chairs.

Neesie handed Bomains a copy of the song and immediately took charge of the practice. "Can you play this song, Bomains?"

"Sure. Do you want me to do a short intro on the guitar before we start singing?"

"Uh, yeah. Go ahead and do an intro. Then you can give me a little nod when it's time to start singing."

Bomains said, "Are you going to lead on the first verse and have me join in on the chorus?"

Neesie said, "Uhhhh, you know what? I don't know. Let's change roles, here. You tell me how we're going to do it and I'll try to come up with ways to improve your ideas. I think that's fair."

Bomains said, "Okay, let's write it down."

Angel found a pen and some paper. "Go ahead, Bomains, I write it down."

"Okay, write this: Intro, first verse Neesie leads, first chorus harmony. Second verse Bomains leads the first two lines, harmony on the second two lines. Chorus harmony, two times. Stop."

Neesie said, "Let's try it and see how it sounds."

Bomains pulled his guitar strap over his shoulder and moved close to Neesie. He said, "Now, Neesie, I want you to think the words as you sing them, and I want you to sing every word from deep down in there, okay? This isn't an in the throat kind of song. This is a straight out of your heart song."

He strummed the guitar. "Ready?"

"Here's the intro."

Bomains began to finger pick a smooth soft melody. He nodded. "Go."

Neesie began.

"The love of God is greater far than tongue or pen can ever tell.

It goes beyond the highest star and reaches to the lowest Hell

The guilty pair, bowed down with care, God gave His Son to win.

His erring child he reconciled, and pardoned from his sin."

Bomains joined in, his voice in harmony with Neesie.

"Oh, love of God, how rich and pure, how measureless and strong!

It shall forevermore endure, the saints and angels' song."

Bomains began his verse.

"Could we with ink the ocean fill, and were the sky of parchment made

Were every stalk on earth a quill, and every man a scribe by trade,"

When Neesie joined for the next two lines, she realized that this was not a children's song.

"To write the love of God above would drain the ocean dry.

Nor could the scroll contain the whole, though stretched from sky to sky!

Oh, love of God! How rich and pure! How measureless and strong!"

Neesie began to sob uncontrollably.

Angel started to come to her, but Bomains put a hand up, motioning for him to stop. "She's okay, Angel. It's the Spirit moving in her."

Neesie said, "I've never even heard this song before, let alone sung it. Oh my heart, it's beautiful."

Bomains said, "Of course, it is. The main part of it was found scribbled on the wall of a cell in an old abandoned insane asylum. Nobody even knows who wrote it."

Neesie said, "Dear Lord, Bomains, I can't sing it!"

Bomais said, "Oh, yes you can. You're not only going to sing it, you're going to live it while you sing it. You're going to sing it while it breaks your heart. And your voice is going to grow stronger the more it hurts. We may have to start over a dozen times before we make it through the whole song, but you are going to sing about The Love of God."

"Let me know when you're ready and we'll start at the beginning again. Neesie, don't hold back. Sing it, girl."

Chapter Forty One

HOMECOMING SUNDAY CAME AND THE church was
packed. The name of the Gospel group was Stronger
Than Water. They were a traditional quartet, two
women and two men. They were very well known in the
Cedar Ridge area and in high demand. The church was
lucky to have them. After an opening prayer, they sang
a few songs and then the preacher gave his homecoming
sermon. It was a rousing message about those who had
gone home and the joy of the moment when we finally
rest from our journey. The preacher had a good sense
of timing. Twenty minutes was long enough to bring
the Word.

Everyone ate lunch. Those close to Neesie and
Bomains were excited. Nobody had heard them except
Angel, and when anyone asked him how they sounded
together, he would always say, "Pretty good."

Bomains introduced Neesie's family to his mother and father. "Dad, this is my boss man, Boots, and his wife, Rachel. And this is Neesie and Angel."

Boots said, "I'm glad to meet you, Mister Grammercy," and reached to shake hands.

Bomains' dad raised his trembling hand about an inch. That was as far as he could move it. Boots patted the man on the shoulder instead. He said, "You've got a fine son, sir. He is a pleasure to have around."

Bomains' dad mumbled something that sounded like "Thank you." Mrs. Grammercy smiled and said, "He's not having a very good day, but we are so excited to be here. Thank you for inviting our son to sing."

Boots said, "It's a blessing to have you and I hope you consider this to be the first homecoming to your new home church."

Stronger Than Water sang for about an hour. The lead singer said, "Church, we need to take a few minutes and get a drink of water. I believe we have a couple of young folks who want to sing, so we'll leave our microphones on. We'll be back in just a few minutes to sing for a little while longer and then we'll wrap it up." The group stepped off of the stage and into a nearby classroom where they had drinks waiting for them.

Bomains allowed the group to get completely out before he and Angel lifted Neesie up on the stage while she was still in her wheelchair. She rolled over to the microphones, and Bomains adjusted one to the right height for Neesie. He got his guitar ready and stepped up to a microphone beside her. He said, "Good afternoon, church. I'm sure most of y'all know Miss Neesie Daws, and I'm Bomains Grammercy. We have one song to sing today and we hope it blesses your souls." He looked at Neesie and said, "Ready?"

Neesie swallowed and nodded. Bomains said, "Here goes," and began to pick the intro on his guitar.

Neesie spread her hands in front of her shoulders and sang every word from her heart.

"The love of God is greater far than tongue or pen can ever tell"

She raised one hand towards the ceiling for the next line.

"It goes beyond the highest star and reaches to the lowest hell

The guilty pair bowed down with care, God gave his son to win

His erring child He reconciled, and pardoned from his sin."

Neesie raised both hands as Bomains' voice joined her in the chorus.

"Oh, love of God! How rich and pure! How measureless and strong!"

Shouts of "Amen," began to come from the congregation. The lead singer for the quartet in the other room stood up from his chair. He said, "Listen.....listen. Who is that?"

All of the group stood. They opened the door, not peeking through a crack, but standing there openly amazed. One of them said, "It's just two kids! How are they doing that?"

The leader said, "That's more than talent. Those two have been anointed by God!"

Bomains began his verse.

"Could we with ink the ocean fill, and were the sky of parchment made

Were every stalk on earth a quill and every man a scribe by trade,"

Neesie raised her hands and she raised her voice to match Bomains'

"To write the love of God above would drain the ocean dry,

Nor could the scroll contain the whole, though stretched from sky to sky!"

The entire congregation stood, shouting praises to God and waving their hands. Bomains' father sat trembling, openly weeping, his wife's arms around him with tears running down her cheeks as well.

"Oh, love of God! How rich and pure! How measureless and strong!

It shall forevermore endure the saints and angels' songs!"

Bomains motioned for the quartet to join them. They gladly ran out of the room and on to the stage. Together, they sang the chorus again.

"Oh, love of God! How rich and pure! How measureless and strong!

It shall forevermore endure, the saints and angels' songs!"

Bomains said, "Sing it again!"

They all sang the chorus again, and the congregation joined in. There were shouts of "Glory!" And many praises were called out to God. Long after the song had ended, the people stood on their feet praying.

Neesie looked up at Bomains and said, "What do we do?"

Bomains said, "Let's be still. I don't know."

The quartet leader stepped behind Bomains and said, "Children, y'all done opened the doors of Heaven today."

Finally, people began to sit back down on the pews. When everyone was seated again, many wiping their eyes with tissue, Bomains said, "Neesie and I thank you for letting us sing today. Please pray for us that we will always follow where the Spirit of God leads."

Bomains set his guitar against the wall. Angel came over to help him move Neesie's wheelchair down. When she was safely down and Angel was pushing her back to her place, Bomains ran to his father and mother. He leaned down and whispered to his dad, holding his trembling hands. He stood and embraced his mother. She smiled and gave him a quick kiss on the cheek.

The quartet sang a few more songs, but even to them the rest of the service was a joy filled blur.

Summer eased by, as summers always do. Mornings started warm and turned hot. An occasional afternoon thundershower did little to cool the evenings, but they did keep the garden watered. The vine crops did very well, and since Laura Dell and Rachel were the only ones who planted cucumbers and watermelons, they sold almost everything they raised at a good price.

Neesie and Angel spent hours and hours at the pool as her back and legs grew stronger. They discussed leaving the wheelchair at home when the time for returning to school approached. Neesie believed she could handle one day without it, but a whole week may be too much of a challenge. Plus, she feared being bumped around while changing classes. The one thing she didn't want to do was to get up out of the wheelchair, only to have to return to it.

As August and Summer wound down to an end, she decided to stay in the wheelchair and keep the fact that she could walk a secret.

As Angel broke the dam of the swimming pool, she stood on the bank and said, "This is our senior year, and I don't need anything on my mind but graduating. After this year, I know that everything will be new to us. The wheelchair doesn't get to go when we start the next part of our lives, Angel."

Angel said, "Yeah."

He didn't say it, but he knew that he probably wouldn't get to go with her, either.

Chapter Forty Two

THEIR SENIOR YEAR OF HIGH school was almost uneventful. Neesie, Angel, and Bomains did much of their work together. Sometimes Bomains would come to Angel's house after the store closed to work on class projects. None of them had exceptional grades, but they were never in danger of failing, either.

Bomains, now a known musician, often spent Saturday nights playing with The Garage Band. He gave them suggestions about how to make their show more entertaining, how to place each member on the stage to give the best appearance, what clothes to wear to project the right image for the group.

He said, "The Garage Band sounds like a bunch of guys having fun playing and singing while their friends dance. So, let's dress like we want to have fun and let's sing good time dance songs with an occasional love song mixed in."

The boys in the group agreed and they played songs that were fun to practice, giving their own flare to the tunes. Bomains was featured in only a few pieces, ballads and old folk songs. A couple of guys would sing harmony where they were needed, but Bomains was practically singing solo on his songs.

With him in the band playing lead guitar and singing an occasional song, the group was getting a lot of opportunities to play. Between Thanksgiving and New Year's Night, they played every Friday and Saturday night.

Angel worked at the store on Saturdays and continued to help Neesie with her exercises and massages. After the first of the new year, they moved their exercise routine to Angel's dance room. Every afternoon, as soon as school was out, Neesie, Angel, and Shady would go into the dance room and close the door. Music would be heard, and the sound of stepping feet made a rhythmic thump, thump, thump throughout the old farm house. After about an hour or sometimes a little bit longer, they would come out, sweaty and tired looking. They would bundle up and go to Neesie's house where Angel would give her a massage.

Sometimes, if the weather was very cold or damp, they would sit by a window and drink a cup of hot chocolate before Angel headed home for the night. By March, they had a new secret. Once again, Rachel noticed them holding hands and whispering. Neesie was all smiles. Angel was as silent as a bank vault. His face told nothing.

Whatever the exercise program was, it produced results. Neesie soon had the body of a gymnast. Angel's shoulders broadened and his arms and legs were thicker.

Still, she kept the wheelchair. She deliberately wore loose clothing, hiding the newly developed muscles in her legs. Even Bomains didn't know she could walk.

At school, their lunch table, which had almost seemed like an invisible prison cell to them for years, became a hub of constant activity. Band members and other musicians discussed music with Bomains. Girls and boys, drawn to Neesie's beauty and bubbly personality, gathered around with happy chatter. Angel sat in his usual chair next to Neesie and across the table from Bomains, perfectly content and glad to see his friends accepted and admired by the other students.

It is the nature of a high school senior to be confident and anxious all in one deep breath. The first great goal in their young lives is almost accomplished. The next great challenge has not yet appeared. Childhood is slipping away like a comfortable pair of shoes that are so worn out that they have to be discarded. Adulthood awaits, barely out of sight, and not a one of the students knows what it really is. So, confidence and humility, pride and worry, are all mixed together like a bowl of alphabet soup, spelling words in a foreign language. They recognize the letters, but they do not know what the word "graduated" means. April approaches. And May will surely follow with all of the ceremonial activities that kindly and beautifully allow the schools to push the people they have helped to create out with a piece of a paper and a wave, "Bye. Don't come back next year."

And, of course, before they graduated there was the one final act. Neesie meant to have her moment of triumph. She had earned it, and she wanted to make a spectacular exit from her wheelchair bound life.

One morning in early May, she brought a CD to school and handed it to Bomains.

"This is the song Angel and I will dance to in this year's talent show. You will use the sound track on here, but you will sing the song. I want you to get a couple of your buddies to sing harmony. I want the best you can get."

Bomains put the CD in his pocket. He smiled and said, "I can do it. Do we need to do anything besides sing?"

Neesie said, "Yeah, dress nice. Y'all will be on the stage while we are dancing."

Bomains looked at Angel who seemed to not be listening. Bomains knew that he was. He wondered how they would dance with Neesie in a wheelchair, but he didn't think it was appropriate to ask. He sensed a secret was being kept, and he wondered why he was left out of the scheme.

"That Angel," he thought. "It's one mystery after another with him."

While Bomains had only a couple of weeks to practice the song, Neesie and Angel had been practicing their dance routine for weeks. They had arranged the dance room exactly as the stage would be set up. They played the sound track over and over and over. Each move must be precise. Neesie could not risk a fall, not with her back completely healed for the first time in fifteen years.

Shady had her part in the dance as well. It was only a small part, but neither Neesie nor Angel thought it was right to leave her out of the act. Angel made her an outfit to wear so she would match the dancers.

Bomains picked a couple of boys from The Garage Band to sing with him. They were all going to be at the talent show anyway. The Garage Band was planning to sing the Eagles' great hit, Hotel California. Bomains would play lead guitar, but he didn't sing at all in the song. He explained to the other singers that since it was a dance routine which Angel had created, they must sing the song exactly as the original group sang it. Their timing must be just like the original.

Neesie informed the principal that she and Angel would be dancing in the talent show and if he didn't mind, would he please let them be the last act?

The principal said, "I expected you to ask for Bomains and The Garage Band to be last, so this is another curve you have thrown at me."

Neesie said, "Bomains and a couple of boys from the band will be singing while we dance, so he gets to perform twice. His feelings won't be hurt. Can you make it work?"

The principal gave Neesie a sad smile. He said, "This school is going to miss y'all next year. It has been our privilege to be your teachers. I'll make it work, and God bless you all."

The night before the talent show, there was an on stage rehearsal. Neesie showed Bomains where he and the other two boys were to stand at the front right side of the stage. She said, "Now, I want you to face the audience until the last chorus, and then you turn and watch us dance while you sing, okay?"

Bomains stood facing the seats and turned, not putting his back to the audience, but far enough that he could plainly see the rest of the stage. "Like this? Is this far enough?"

"That's about right. Now, let us get ready, and then you can start singing." She wheeled herself over to the other side of the stage where Angel was waiting. They talked for a second. Angel lifted Neesie out of the wheelchair and sat her on a small bench that was against the wall. He pushed the wheelchair back out of the way and came over and stood near Neesie.

Neesie said, "Go ahead, Bomains. We're ready."

The music started. Bomains and the boys sang the song as Angel danced around the stage with Neesie in his arms. Shady jumped up on a bench and sat and watched the couple as they danced.

Just before they started singing the last course, Neesie called, "Okay, turn!" And the singers turned to watch Angel waltz around the stage with Neesie in his arms until the music stopped. Neesie said, "That's it. Thanks, guys, see you tomorrow night."

Angel carried her to the wheelchair and they were gone.

Bomains wondered what was going on. The dance was beautiful. Anyone could watch Angel dance all day and be impressed with his ability, but he couldn't see Neesie getting on stage and being carried around by Angel and calling it a dance. There was something he didn't see when his back was turned. What was it?

Chapter Forty Three

THURSDAY NIGHT CAME. THE CLOCK had seemed to turn slower and slower until five o'clock. As soon as Neesie and Angel arrived at the auditorium, everything became a blur. There were fifteen acts this year. The quality of performers increased with every act. The Garage Band was twelfth in line and they were spectacular. Bomains' rift on the guitar in Hotel California brought a huge applause from the audience.

Ace Kyker was home for the summer. He stood with his chin hanging loose as Bomains worked the strings of his guitar. "I thought he said he wasn't ready for rock and roll," he said to nobody in particular. "Bomains, you lied to me."

When the Garage Band finished their number, Ace was one of the loudest to cheer. He knew they were good and he saw a rare talent in Bomains. That boy could go somewhere with a decent manager.

There were two more acts and then the stage went dark. The curtains closed as the props were brought in for the final entry to the talent show. Bomains and his fellow singers arranged themselves at the front of the stage, just behind the closed curtains.

The stage hands brought a small bed to the middle of the stage and placed it at an angle to the audience. A sheer white curtain was hung on an eight feet wide by eight feet tall frame behind the farthest end of the bed. There was a chair set against the far side of the stage. Neesie was sitting in the chair with Shady in her lap. Neesie was wearing a beautiful sparkling white silk gown. The hem landed just above her knees as she sat. Shady was dressed in white silk as well. She sat still in Neesie's lap. Angel wore a white tuxedo with navy blue piping. Of course, he wore a top hat. He stood a few steps back on the stage from Neesie.

The Master of Ceremonies spoke, "Ladies and gentlemen! Singing Dream On, Gareth Bomains Grammercy, and dancing The Waltz of the Angels, Miss Denise Daws and her partner, Michael Angelo Higgins!"

The lights on stage came on, the curtain opened, and the intro music began. Angel, stepping in time with the music, moved to Neesie and lifted her from the chair and began to waltz around with her in his arms. He held one arm around her back and ribs while the other forearm supported her legs just above her knees. As he began to dance, Shady took two hops and landed at the end of the little bed and curled up as if she were asleep. Bomains began to sing.

"Lay your head down on my shoulder, I won't let the night get colder."

Neesie wrapped her arms around Angel's neck and laid her head against his chest. He danced as Bomains sang.

"I'll protect you, I'll be keeping trouble far from where you're sleeping.

Until you wake in the morning, you've got the world to yourself."

Angel waltzed, spinning Neesie around and around in smooth graceful circles. She held on tightly, try not to get dizzy.

"Dream on! Dream about the world we're gonna live in one fine day.

Dream on! Spend the night in Heaven, I'll be here to light your way.

Someday tomorrow we'll smile, but little girl in the meanwhile,"

Angel had danced around to place himself next to the little bed. He lay Neesie gently down on her back and kissed her on the forehead and stepped away as Bomains and his boys sang the last words of the chorus.

"Dream on."

Here, there was a very short musical interlude as Angel approached the bed again where Neesie lay. As she raised one hand in a smooth motion, Angel took it in his. Bomains began to sing again.

"You're a princess, chains around you."

Angel lifted her into his arms as he had done before.

"I'm a hero who just found you."

Angel danced a long circle, staying on the far side of the stage.

"Till a brand new day must wake you, let imagination take you."

Angel raised Neesie as high as he could, her knees against his chest as he wrapped his arms around her thighs. She waved her hands out and then inward until they touched with her arms extended straight above her head. Then, as they passed behind the sheer curtain and only their silhouettes could be seen, Angel seemed to stumble, falling to one knee. The crowd gasped as Neesie appeared to be thrown from his arms! She came into clear sight of the audience, whirling and dancing on her own feet as Bomains, unable to see what had happened sang.

"Go where the music is playing!"

Girls' voices could be heard screaming in the audience.

"I'll be along in a while."

Neesie whirled again and again, her arms and hands a constantly changing in smooth patterns around her. The short silk gown showed her beautiful muscular legs as Bomains continued to sing.

"Dream on! Dream about the world we're gonna live in one fine day.

Dream on! Spend the night in heaven, I'll be here to light your way."

Angel caught her in perfect step and time. They waltzed in wide, beautiful circles. Neesie matched his long strides, her head tilted back, her hand on his shoulder in classic ballroom form. They were the very essence of power and grace as they covered the stage floor in time to Bomains' voice.

"Someday tomorrow we'll smile, but little girl in the meanwhile

Dream on."

Bomains turned as he had been told and saw them dancing for the first time. Neesie was dancing with Angel! On her strong, beautiful legs, she was dancing!

"Dream on! Dream about the world we're gonna live in one fine day!

Dream on! Spend the night in Heaven, I'll be here to light your way.

Someday tomorrow we'll smile, but little girl in the meanwhile

Dream on!"

As the final musical notes faded, Angel and Neesie wound up stopping next to Bomains, just as they had practiced.

Forgetting to turn off his microphone, Bomains shouted, "Neesie, you can walk! Neesie you can dance!" His voice cracked, hindered by the lump in his throat.

He ran to Angel and bear hugged him. "You did it, Angel! You made a miracle happen! You made Neesie walk!"

Finally, for one of the few times in his life, Angel grinned. "Angel has helped Neesie walk in Jesus! Amen."

Bomains and Neesie hugged Angel and each other.

The crowd was standing on their feet, clapping their hands and cheering. Almost all of the students had known Neesie in a wheelchair, Bomains quiet and lonely, practically friendless, and Angel autistic and silent, the guardian of a little cripple girl in a wheelchair. Now, there they were, as far as they could go in their school.

They stood on the stage and waved to their friends and teachers. "Good bye, Cedar Ridge High School! Our time here has ended. We leave you with a miracle. Remember when you are struggling, when you are lonely, when you don't seem to fit in, something wonderful is waiting just around the corner. Always keep believing. You'll have your chance one day to dance with an Angel!"

A Few Final Thoughts

MY KNOWLEDGE OF AUTISTIC CHILDREN is limited to the few who I have known personally in my life. Those who are high functioning often have one amazing talent and that is what I focused on with Angel, his hand and eye coordination as well as his ability to organize.

The struggle to find an autistic child's mind and help him learn to function in society is a complicated heartbreaking effort for both parent and child. Improvements are small and sometimes barely noticeable.

Many children who have lived in family tragedy are often silent and socially awkward. Their entire lives can become private, not even shared with the few friends they do find. Sometimes a special person comes along and becomes a confidant and adviser, making a good change in the child's life. The relationship that developed between Boots and Bomains is an example of a friendship that happens more often than we know.

An early life injury that puts a child in a physically disabled situation for a long period of time can cause emotional pain which manifests itself through doubt and frustration. A child with a strong spirit will find a way to enjoy life and hold on to the hope of recovery for a long, long time. Occasionally we hear of someone who has overcome a severe injury against all odds. Of these children, I believe we could start a list, and it would be surprisingly long. Neesie, happy, hopeful, and beautiful, is an example of one of those little warriors who are determined to recover their natural physical strength.

All of the parents are just Moms and Dads being what they have to be. They adjust to whatever a day brings, living within the circumstances of life. They provide hope, humor, effort, and wisdom. Between the moments of tragic misery, they create days and years of happiness for their children.

The most common virtue, shared by parents and children alike, is an unshakable faith in the great Creator. It is from God, who they can not see or hear, that they draw strength to face day after day of slow learning, physical pain, and personal loneliness.

When a miracle does happen, whether suddenly or after a long cycle of recovery, it is almost a natural truth that the children are not surprised. There are few things more spiritually powerful than the faith of a child.

The farm at Easy Creek doesn't exist anywhere in the real world, but I have been there many times in my dreams. It is where I live when I am asleep. The old farmhouse, the apple tree and the rusty gate, the path along the edge of the field and the slow flowing creek, the little streams coming down the side of the ridge, and the big shady oak are there. I hope you have enjoyed your visit.

As for the most likely question to be asked, here is the explanation of the name Bomains.

In the time of King Arthur, there was a boy who worked in the kitchen at the castle. He was treated badly by Sir Key, his supervisor. Sir Key called him Beaumains, which was an insult, meaning Clumsy or Big Hands. Beaumains worked faithfully and never complained. Sir Lancelot became angry about how the boy was treated.

One day, Beaumains was secretly given a horse and some armor. He jousted with Sir Key and defeated him. Sir Lancelot dubbed him a knight, and the humble, clumsy kitchen helper became Sir Gareth a knight of the round table. Sir Gareth, however, preferred his nickname and called himself Sir Beaumains and only the knights ever knew his true identity.

Grammercy is an ancient request that an injured knight would ask of an opposing knight if he were injured in a sporting joust, or of a local resident after a hard battle during war. So, the translated name of our Bomains is Merciful Knight.

As always, I ask only this as you remember the friends you have known in this book. When you feel like you are completely beaten, when the hard part of life has won and you think that there is not an ounce of strength left in you, remember us and get up and try one more time. Call out to your Creator and see if he has a miracle waiting for you.

Ask and you shall receive. Angel will help you walk again in Jesus.

Amen.

Cover Photographs

Angel	Tyler Evans (Autistic)
Neesie	Lorelai
Bomains	Kyler Brown
Shady	Kela Allcock of Texas

About The Author

A NATIVE SON OF THE Appalachian foothills of North Alabama, Dan was born in Jacksonville, the eighth child in a family of twelve children. His father died when he was seven years old, and his family struggled through years of poverty. Yet, while they seemed to be needful of physical items, the family was full of humor and hope and love.

Dan spent his childhood playing along the rocky ridges of Crooked Mountain. He learned the nature of animals, and he knew them. The hawks, foxes, and snakes did not hide what they were. In the wilderness, there is a simple honesty.

But when he walked in ragged clothes along the smooth streets of his hometown, a different system of life was learned. People weren't so obvious about their intentions. The rules of society are complex and usually unspoken. There is only one Nature, but the human natures are uncountable. So learning to understand people takes a few years. To Dan, understanding people may be accomplished only if he counts them by ones. In each life is a single adventure.

After a lifetime of bumping into other people's tears and trophies, Dan has become one of those rare and wonderful story tellers. From his first inspirational tale, *The Owls of Thunder Hollow*, to this, the story of an autistic little boy who finds his family, his friends, and his purpose in life, Dan's soul-deep narratives make the readers feel like they are lost in the woods after dark, and it's a long walk home.

You open the book and fall in. Once the story begins, there's no way out except by the final page. Along the way, Dan weaves around you a wonderful and heart felt mystery.

Other Books by Dan Barnwell:

The Owls of Thunder Hollow

The Fire in Thunder Hollow

The Tree in Thunder Hollow

The Jelly Tree

The Goldenrod

The Untimely Death of the Old Gray Soldier

Foothill Fables

A Fox in the Devil's Rockyard

This book is a work of fiction. People, places, events, and situations are the product of the author's imagination. Any resemblance to actual persons, living or dead, or historical events is purely coincidental.

Made in the USA
Columbia, SC
12 August 2022

64768531R00162